Nesthäkchen and Her Dolls

Nesthäkchen and Her Dolls

By Else Ury

First English edition of the German Children's Classic

Translated and annotated by Steven Lehrer

SF Tafel Publishers

New York

First SF Tafel International Edition, July 2016
English Translation Copyright © 2016 by Steven Lehrer
All rights reserved under International and Pan-American Copyright Conventions.
Published in the United States by SF Tafel, New York
Originally published in Germany as *Nesthäkchen und ihre Puppen* by Else Ury,
Meidingers Jugendschriften Verlag, Berlin, 1913.
This translation first published in trade paper in the United States by SF Tafel,
New York, 2016.
Ury, Else, 1877–1943
Steven Lehrer (translator)
Translation of: *Nesthäkchen und ihre Puppen*
ISBN-13: 978-1530642007
ISBN-10: 1530642000
Summary: Relates the fictional adventures of Nesthäkchen, a young German girl,
before World War I.
Series: Nesthäkchen; Bd. 1
Ury, Else, 1877-1943. Nesthäkchen; Bd. 1.
School children--Germany--Fiction.
Girls--Germany--Fiction.
Genre/Form: Adventure stories.
Subjects--Germany--Juvenile fiction.
Nesthäkchen (Fictitious character)--Juvenile fiction.
Library of Congress Control Number: 2016936549

SF Tafel Publishers
30 West 60th Street
New York, New York 10023-7909
http://sftafel.com

The human heart is like the soil, often hard and brittle. One must sow the seeds of love, patiently cherish and care for them, as for any other plant, so that the roots will take hold and thrive.

Else Ury

Contents

Chapter 1.
Little Doll Mother

Have you ever seen our Nesthäkchen?

She's Annemarie, but Father and Mom call her mostly "Lotte." Our Nesthäkchen has a funny pug nose and two tiny blond pigtails with large, bright blue ribbons. "Rat-tails" brother Hans calls Annemarie's braids, but the little one is immensely proud of them. Sometimes Nesthäkchen wears pink hair ribbons, and the pigtails stick like cute, small buns to each ear. But she can not stand this hairstyle, because the old hairpins prick her. Annemarie recently turned six years old. Both her legs are covered by knee length stockings in which she hops around. Not for a moment does she or her cherry red mouth stand still. She chatters and questions the livelong day, laughing, singing, but rarely crying.

So our youngest looks, and if you live in Berlin, you can see her go to the Tiergarten Park every day with Fräulein. Annemarie lives in an elegant, large home on a long street, along which rolls the electrified railway. A garden is in front of the home, but the doorman allows no one inside. He himself often walks around in it, as he must cut the grass, water the flower beds and paint the trellis with new oil paint. Annemarie believes that the porter is nearly as important as the Emperor. And if she were not Mommy's youngest, she would like to be the porter best of all; but sometimes the pastry baker.

Annemarie has two brothers, the wild Klaus, who is two years older than she, and the magnificent middle school student Hans, who knows Latin. Hänschen loves the girl, but he often times teases her along with brother Kläuschen.

Oh, what a nice warm nest, Nesthäkchen's home. When tired, Father comes home from his practice. Annemarie's Papa is a busy doctor. When his girl jumps jubilantly onto his neck, he forgets all fatigue. He laughs and jokes with her, yes, he even puts the jubilant thing on his shoulders and rides with her through all the rooms.

Mommy says: "You are spoiling our Lotte, Father, she is far too large for that." Whereupon he presses his favorite more firmly to his heart and says with a smile: "she's our smallest."

But if Father assumes it will soon be time for Annemarie to start school, Mommy spreads her arms around her daughter and asks: "Leave her with me for a while at home; she is so delicate and our youngest withal."

Yes, Nesthäkchen gets a bit of pleasure from both sides. Her Fräulein may have much to do, but she is never so tired that she cannot answer Annemie's thousands of questions. Fräulein is terribly fond of the girl.

Hanne, the cook, chuckles and her wide, red face beams when Annemie comes into the kitchen. Alone, Hanne gets bored. The little lady rummages among Hanne's pots, spoons and eggbeaters, but Hanne doesn't kick Annemarie out. In contrast, she has little patience with the two brothers, and expels them from her domain posthaste.

Even Frida, the maid, enjoys Nesthäkchen's society when ironing, using her sewing machine, or waxing floors.

The good brother Hans, despite his demanding schoolwork, makes time to build model boats and tops with his sister.

Klaus thinks that Annemie is spoiled and wants a stricter upbringing. Most of his interaction with her ends pugilistically.

Puck, the cute dwarf pooch, and Antics, the canary, show a particular fondness for Nesthäkchen. Puck is patient when she tousles his ears and tail and is a participant in her games. Antics sings jubilantly in competition with her.

But who do you suppose is Annemarie's favorite? Her parents, Father and Mommy, of course, and in next place her dolls.

The dolls smile from ear to ear, filled with joy, as soon as the girl enters the nursery. What a good doll mother Annemie is. Every child of her large doll family embraces her in its tender heart.

First there is Irenchen; she's the eldest. She has a satchel with slate and writing implements. Irenchen worries her little Mama. She lost her pretty rosy cheeks after Nesthäkchen scrubbed her face with pumice. When the doll child wrote for the first time with ink, she stuck her nose deep into the exercise book. Repeatedly she smeared it with ink, that thoughtless Irenchen, and sullied the white apron of her small mom, too. Annemarie scolded Irenchen and Fräulein scolded Annemie. Fräulein began to work with lemon on Annemarie's inky apron. Annemie worked on the inky face of her Irenchen with pumice. Oh that hurt! Irenchen screamed like a stuck pig. Nesthäkchen energetically rubbed because "whoever does not listen must feel." The poor doll child is still quite pale and Annemie has expressed her concern to Fräulein: "I think the school air does not agree with the child."

Annemarie cares for her second daughter, Mariannchen. The doll has had a serious eye disease for a few days and must soon visit a doll clinic. Her sleepy eyes are firmly glued shut and no longer open. Worst is that little Mummy herself is to blame for the disease. Or rather, Klaus; he advised her to pour liquid glue on the child's lashes. Mariannchen's eyes are gelatinized, or rather "festered" as the four-legged Doctor Puck noted with thoughtful tail wagging.

Yes indeed, the doll mother has her worries. The doll boy Kurt is terribly wild. No table is too high for him to jump off. He has smashed his nose, has a deep hole in his head, and has already knocked off half a foot, the rascal.

The bravest is Baby. He allows his mom to sleep all night peacefully. He cries during the daytime, but only when he is pressed too much in the abdomen. Annemie has slightly disfigured Baby, but he's her youngest.

Despite all her mistakes Annemarie loves her children like a proper mummy. All day long she toils for them. She brings Irenchen to school early in the morning and dresses the others. Then baby needs his bottle.

She proceeds to make the beds of the children. The two biggest dolls sleep in the white canopy bed. The two small ones, Lolo, a Moor doll, and Baby, sleep in the wagon. Kurt sleeps on the overturned footstool. At least it's not as high if he falls out.

When Fräulein cleans up the nursery, Nesthäkchen helps diligently. She has a small broom, a shovel and a scrub brush along with a bucket and scouring-cloth. Annemie likes washing up, but Fräulein does not allow it often, because the whole room ends up under water; there is inevitably a flood. The other day her Kurt, who was hiding under the game cabinet, almost drowned.

Annemarie has a lovely doll kitchen. She cooks with a coal box, running water and an alcohol stove, but she can make lunch bread for her children only when it rains. The dolls are sensible enough not to be hungry in fine weather. They know that their mama, when the sun shines, must walk in the Tiergarten. Often Nesthäkchen takes out one or two of her children in their spiffy white doll carriage with pink silk blanket. Then she puts in front of them spinach, freshly picked from the lawn. They tolerate pebble roast remarkably well, although it is tough.

The poor ones left behind have their garden, the flower board on the window sill, where they can grab a bit of air. Kurt, the villain, is too wild and would certainly somersault into the yard.

Annemarie must wash and iron for her children. Yes, she occasionally burns her hands in her zeal. The small iron is heated on the stove; otherwise the house mother does not deign to use it.

Soon the dolls will have a tailor. Annemarie received for her birthday a charming small sewing machine. Fräulein wants to show her how to sew.

She has the grocery store and the flour store to visit when Klaus does not feel like going, or if they have quarreled.

Mom likes her Nesthäkchen's company. Annemarie often does not know what to do first. It's hard to believe that there are little girls who become bored.

Chapter 2.
What the Easter Bunny brings

It was Easter Sunday, early in the morning. Golden shined the dear sun in the sky, right into Nesthäkchen's nursery.

The dolls were fast asleep. Kurt was snoring like a log. Lotte and Fräulein were still asleep.

Oops, the sun began to blink in astonishment. What should that mean?

From the white crib in the corner, a child with two blond pigtails jumped warily past the sleeping Fräulein. One, two, three, she slipped quietly across the room, straight to the window, and climbed gently onto the high chair.

Why did Nesthäkchen have to peep down into the yard at the crack of dawn? The porter's children, with whom she was good friends, were asleep.

The sun made a disapproving face. Death could call the barefooted little thing in this early game, or at least a bad cold.

No, the dear sun did not want to see Annemarie sick in bed during the Easter holidays. The sun quickly beamed a couple of sharp gold rays, which began to crawl under the nose of Fräulein, once and once again.

"Achoo," sneezed Fräulein and opened her eyes. She saw to her amazement at the window, enthroned on the high chair, a child bent over, pug nose pressed against the pane.

"Child, Annemie, will you please come right back to bed, it's not even six yet," she shouted angrily.

"Ah, Fräulein," Annemarie said startled, "why did you wake up? I wanted terribly to see the Easter Bunny. He has quite a lot of eggs for me."

"If you're so naughty and secretly climb out of bed, the Easter bunny brings you no eggs. He only comes to good children. Jump back in bed, Annemie, so you don't get ill," warned Fräulein.

"How does the Easter Bunny know if I'm good?" inquired the barefoot girl.

"He gets the info from all Mums and Fräuleins," said Fräulein.

"Did he ask you?"

"Yes ma'am," Fräulein yawned heartbreakingly.

"When?" Nesthäkchen perked up her ears.

"Stop with the eternal questions and go back to bed, Annemie, or should I just get angry?"

"No, no, but my favorite, best, all sweetest, sugar Fräulein, tell me, when was the Easter Bunny here. Then, well-behaved, I go right back to bed," coaxed the girl.

"Last night." Fräulein could not resist the pleas of the cuddly kitten.

"Last night? You talked to him in your sleep, Fräulein?" marveled the girl.

Annemie wanted to retreat into her crib. But she suddenly shouted out so loudly that all the dolls in horror vaulted from sleep, and Kurt was almost bowled from his footstool in fright.

"Fräulein, the Easter Bunny, I clearly saw him."

The child pointed excitedly out the window. "He was black and had a long tail. With one bound he jumped over the roof. "

"You little sheep, that was the black cat of our porter," laughed Fräulein.

"The cat? Nonsense, that was the Easter Bunny." Annemie could not easily put the subject to rest. As she lay back in bed and closed her tired blue eyes, she mumbled in her sleep: "It was the Easter Bunny."

For a while, as the dear sun looked into the nursery, it was quiet. As the whole society slept, the Easter Bunny could, unobserved by curious children's eyes, hide his chocolate and marzipan eggs.

It was difficult for Fräulein to dress Nesthäkchen. The tomboy was never quiet, but today Annemarie was in all four corners of the nursery at the same time. In the end, Fräulein had not paid attention, and the Easter Bunny left a few eggs in the nursery.

While Fräulein untangled Annemarie's blond curly hair, never a pleasant task, she escaped her coiffeuse three times.

Whoosh, she was in the shoe closet, where she ransacked all the shoes and boots for Easter eggs. Fräulein followed after her with brush and comb.

As half her hair was braided, Annemie became sure she would find something in the play kitchen.

Zoom, she rummaged there, bottom to top, Fräulein in hot pursuit with comb and brush.

The girl was being adorned with large, bright blue ribbons when she climbed on the table to peer at the stove for Easter eggs. Fräulein could not reach her with brush and comb. It was impossible for her to climb on the table. She made an unhappy face until Annemie attached herself to Fräulein's neck with kissing and fondling, promising to be polite. She did this because as small as she was, she knew that "Promises must be kept."

"Well, finally rested, Lotte?" Father greeted Nesthäkchen when she appeared at the coffee table.

"Oh, Daddy, I saw the Easter Bunny jump this morning over the roof," Annemarie related eagerly.

"So?" The father asked seriously.

The cheeky Klaus cried: "There is no Easter Bunny; you are a stupid thing, just ordinary rabbits out there."

"That's not true, you're lying!" replied the sister.

Klaus didn't want to hear it. He grabbed Annemarie's freshly braided pigtail. They would probably have come to a real battle this beautiful Easter Sunday if Mommy had not entered the room.

"Oh, children, is this our holiday peace?" she asked accusingly.

The small gamecocks were both ashamed. Nesthäkchen jumped to Mommy to get her good morning kiss.

Are there harder tasks in life than having to drink two large cups of cocoa, while knowing that waiting in the next room are the most beautiful Easter eggs?

At last the second cup was empty. Annemarie could no longer be restrained.

"Mom, can we please, please, search for the Easter eggs?"

Mommy gave her impatient daughter a smidgen of a nod. Nesthäkchen bolted into the living room under the sofa, kicking excitedly with both feet.

"Hurrah hurray, a big piece is under the music cabinet, another one under the flower stand," Annemarie rejoiced. "No, Klaus, I saw it first, that belongs to me!" This time there was no struggle between the two. The magnanimous Hans diligently sought to leave enough eggs for two.

Annemie found a gorgeous green nest and admired the marzipan chicks. The good Father helped; he read the attached piece of paper: "For our Nesthäkchen."

A loud crash: Mommy's beautiful vase had shattered. The head of the impetuous Klaus collided with it. As punishment, he was excluded from the egg hunt and sent to his room.

Nesthäkchen thought secretly: "Surely the Easter bunny has set Klaus up because he said that there is no Easter Bunny."

Annemie no longer felt the joy of the merry search, although she still found many gorgeous eggs, even one with marbles and one filled with pastry. She constantly thought of how sad the poor Klaus was, sitting in his room. He was terribly sorry, terribly, yet he nevertheless always started their disputes.

She left no corner unexamined. Annemarie counted fifteen eggs in her basket, a whole clutch, as Fräulein said.

Annemarie tried to sneak into Klaus' room.

Klaus was sitting at his work desk and had drilled his fists into both eyes.

"Kläuschen," the little one came closer shyly, "look how many eggs I have. I'll take a few because I found a ton. You can have one."

The boy looked up in astonishment. At first he thought Annemie was kidding, but when the good sister held out her basket, he took the egg with the marbles and patted Annemie's round face.

"You're a good guy," he said.

Nesthäkchen could fully enjoy the gifts of the Easter Bunny because Klaus was pleased. Jubilantly the girl danced through the entire apartment.

"Hanne, I have found a whole clutch of eggs," she called out at the kitchen door. The next moment Annemie sprang on Frida sweeping with her broom, and rode her piggyback.

"Fridachen, let me clean a bit with the carpet sweeper. I'll give you one of my fifteen eggs."

But she had no time to wait for Frida's answer because Puck had learned that she had ten chocolate eggs, four of marzipan, one with pastry, and the nest of sweet chicks. The poor creature had been locked up all morning so that he should not seek his own Easter eggs. Should he not have a lick?

"Puckchen, look what I have here." Laughing, Annemarie crouched and held out to the doggie her sweet treasures. But Nesthäkchen's laughter suddenly turned to tears. The thankless Puck was not satisfied by the view. Snap! He had the biggest chocolate egg in his mouth and crept under the sofa.

"You vile Puck!" Annemie raced in tears behind him to snatch his prey from him.

Brother Hans witnessed the bold theft and held his sides with laughter. He pulled out a knee length stocking from under the sofa.

"Let the crazy dog have the Easter egg, Annemie. You can't eat it now," he consoled.

Nesthäkchen's tears continued to flow. The good Hans took one of his own eggs and put it in his sister's basket.

Sunshine enveloped Annemarie. She raced into the nursery to show the dolls her eggs. They wouldn't eat them up.

The doorbell rang.

Mommy had strictly forbidden Annemie to open the front door by herself. Many of the visitors were Father's patients. But the little lady was quite curious. She peeked through the letter slot.

She saw a dark green woman's coat and a hand with a silver-gray bag, which seemed to her strangely familiar.

The hand held a promising package. Nesthäkchen asked softly through the door: "Who's there?"

"The Easter Bunny," replied a disguised voice quietly.

"Frida, quickly, Frida, the Easter Bunny is outside." The girl could not wait until the door had been opened.

The Easter Bunny wasn't waiting outside; instead, a lady who was as dear to Annemie: Grandma.

"Good day, my dear, why don't you let the Easter Bunny in?" Affectionately Grandma picked up the girl.

"Mom does not allow me to open the door, and you are not the Easter Bunny," laughed the grandchild.

"If I'm not a bunny, I can't buy you any eggs," said Grandma, who hid jokingly her package behind her back.

"Oh, you're my dearest, best Easter Bunny, Grandmother. May I see, please, please, what is in the package?"

Annemie reinforced her request with caressing and kissing of Grandma's green jacket.

This blandishment was not necessary. Whoever saw Nesthäkchen's begging blue eyes, Grandmother included, could not resist them.

The girl tore off the stupid wrapping paper. A large box appeared. Half fearful, half expectantly, Nesthäkchen raised the lid.

"A doll, a bunny doll, oh how sweet" Beaming with joy, Annemie took out the large doll that wore a white Easter bunny cap with pink silken ears, and gave her a tender welcome kiss.

"I think you are not pleased with your new daughter; you have too many children," teased Grandmother when she saw Annemie's motherly happiness.

"Oh, Granny, I thank you a thousand times," said Nesthäkchen, filled with gratitude. "This has been my best Easter." Blessedly Grandma stroked the girl's red cheeks, blond curls, white embroidered dress and pink sash.

"Mom, you've got a new grandchild." With one hand Annemarie led Grandmother into the room, with the other she handed Mother the newborn child. Mommy did not know whom she should greet first.

"What will we name my new great granddaughter?" asked Grandma.

"We'll call her Gertrud after Grandma," suggested Mommy.

"Oh no, Gertrud is for old ladies," objected Nesthäkchen.

"So call her Gerda." Mommy always knew a way out.

And that was all. Gerda walked on Annemarie's arm into the nursery and was presented to Fräulein, as well as all her brothers and sisters. That night she was allowed to sleep in her new mom's white crib. Annemarie didn't want to be separated from her for a single moment.

Baby was deposed and Gerda was henceforth Annemie's Nesthäkchen.

Chapter 3.
How Doll Gerda liked it with Nesthäkchen

When Doll Gerda opened her sleepy eyes the next morning, her new mama was asleep. Curious, Gerda observed her mother in more detail. With red cheeks Mamma lay on the embroidered pillows and laughed in her sleep.

Certainly she dreamed of her new child. The pretty Mama liked the doll child and was sure they would have a good time. Gerda made a mental note to always be good and never annoy Annemie. Then she folded her celluloid hands and whispered, "Dear God, I thank thee that thou hast brought me such a good Mother."

Annemarie was asleep, and Doll Gerda got bored.

Surr surr, a fly buzzed on the crib and landed right on the doll's nose.

"Surr surr, how did you get here, Miss?" asked the fly. "I've lived a long life, two whole days in the nursery, but I have not seen you here."

"I arrived yesterday," the doll replied shyly, glancing at the beating heart on her nose. She had never in her life seen a fly.

"Surr surr, where did you live before?" inquired the fly.

"In a large cardboard box, but it was not nearly as pretty as here. It was pitch dark inside, and the air was not particularly good," said Doll Gerda, a bit more trusting. When she saw that the fly meant no harm, she added: "I've done well coming here, no?"

"Sum sum," the fly said for a change, putting one of his thin front legs to his forehead in thought. "Yes, they are quite decent people; they do not skimp on sugar crumb cake and don't hang sticky flypaper on the lamp covers to cause us fidgeting poor flies to lose our lives. Sum sum."

"Is Annemarie a good person?" asked the doll, because that was more important to her than sugar crumbs and fly paper.

"Of course," the fly whirred back, "Annemie would not harm a fly. But watch out for Klaus, her older brother, Miss. He is the most dangerous person I know. If he gets hold of you, he'll crush you to applesauce, or he'll tear off at least one of your legs. The wretch did that to my good old aunt."

"I'll give him a wide berth," the doll replied frightened. "I saw last night another young gentleman. Is he as bad?"

"Sum sum, depends how you look at it! Hans is not quite so bad. But he sometimes has a large, bulbous glass bottle in his hand that attracts us poor flies. The alcohol goes to our heads and we zoom straight into the bottle. Whoever flies in there will not fly back out. The visitor miserably drowns in the alcohol! Beware of the fly bottle, Miss, surr surr."

The indignant fly buzzed so loudly that Nesthäkchen began to move.

Husch, the fly was up and away, and doll Gerda's nose was fly-free.

Annemarie stretched and stretched, and she opened her eyes.

Doll Gerda pondered whether it would not be wisest to take to her heels and run away from the evil big brothers before Annemie awoke. But she felt herself embraced intimately by two soft childish arms. A red mouth pressed to hers, and a warm heart pounded against her cold celluloid body. So loving and affectionate was Annemarie that all Gerda's fear of terrible Klaus and the evil fly bottle vanished. Doll Gerda felt well-guarded and safe beside her mother.

"Good morning, my only Gerdachen. Has my Nesthäkchen slept well?" said Annemarie lovingly.

The doll nodded because her head was attached with elastic cord.

"Should we drink some sweet sugar milk?" asked the caring mother.

Doll Gerda smiled, pleased. She had fierce thirst, and sugar milk was her favorite dish. But she had to wait a bit longer. Fräulein entered the room to fetch Annemarie.

The girl made a face. The stupid getting dressed. She had been looking forward to playing with her Gerda in bed a while longer.

Fräulein bowed down to her and whispered something in her ear. The girl blushed and looked embarrassed at her baby doll.

Had Gerda heard what Fräulein said? Annemarie should not be ashamed in front of her new child, and she must be polite and obedient to set her Gerda a good example.

The doll made an innocent face and looked respectfully at her small mom.

One two three, Annemarie was out of bed. Fräulein should not have rebuked her. Gerda was placed in the bed against the embroidered cushion in the corner and could sit and watch Annemie's bath.

And that was good because Annemie was shy in front of her new child. The doll should not know that her mom occasionally screamed when being washed, especially if the water felt overly wet. The girl ground her teeth together forcefully so that no sound escaped her while Fräulein set the large sponge in motion and disgustingly rubbed. Nesthäkchen emitted only one little "Ow!" during her coiffure, even though the old comb was efficient today. Fräulein immediately gave Doll Gerda a place in her heart. The doll had accomplished miracles.

Gerda was not ashamed of her small mom. When Annemarie found time to dress her, Gerda clamped her cute porcelain teeth together firmly. Annemie rubbed more disgustingly than Fräulein had and tore more forcefully at Gerda's flat golden blond hair. But no, Gerda did not scream; what would the other dolls think?

They weren't friendly to the newcomer, anyway.

"I want to get dressed, I have to go to school, otherwise I will get a reprimand" cried out Irenchen for the third time behind the white curtain of her four-poster bed. But Annemarie had eyes and ears for her Gerda alone.

"Annemie has put no dressing on my bad eyes, although Doctor Puck prescribed one," lamented Mariannchen.

"She does not take care of us. She is focused on the floozie with the blond flat head that arrived yesterday; she kisses her constantly," reported Irenchen, peeping through the white bed curtains, intensely jealous. "I have much nicer braids."

"How does the new doll look? Is she pretty?" Mariannchen inquired earnestly. All too happily she would have had her glued eyes opened to look at Doll Gerda.

"I think she looks quite ordinary," Irenchen said contemptuously, "She has red cheeks like a peasant girl. If you want to be posh, you have to be as pale as I am."

The occupants of the white doll carriage murmured.

Lolo, the Moor's child, pushed the carriage curtain with her rigid porcelain hand slightly to one side to get a better look. It was outrageous that Annemarie washed and combed the newborn but paid no attention to her. Hotheaded Lolo stomped her feet against the inside of the carriage.

"My dress apron, my pretty Sunday apron, she's tying it on that animal. She won't get away with pinching my apron." Lolo cried so loudly that Baby beside her in her pixie suit opened her eyes and puckered her whiny mouth.

"Mama Mama," cried Baby, "I want my bottle with sweet sugar milk."

Annemarie didn't hear the crying and yelling of her children. The girl was feeding Gerda the sweet sugar milk, which baby got otherwise.

"Does it taste good to you, my Gerdachen?" she asked carefully, adding an additional spoonful of sugar from the doll's kitchen.

The doll shook her head.

No, it did not taste good, but she liked to drink sugar milk. Annemie had poured it in her best pink cup with a gold rim. How could Gerda drink it? Baby was constantly crying out for her sugar milk? Lolo grumbled about her stolen Sunday apron that Annemie had covered with milk splotches. Irenchen was in a huff, and screamed that she intended to remain at school today. Gerda would have preferred to cover her ears so as not to hear all the ugly words being bandied about. But she could not, although she was a doll with flexible joints.

Gerda was stiff. She no longer wanted to drink the poor, thirsty Baby's sugar milk. Leave a bit for the kid. But Annemarie was a strict mother.

"If you do not finish your milk, you will not be big and strong, my favorite," she said in the same tone of voice Mom used when Annemie herself sometimes did not want to drink her cocoa.

Doll Gerda obeyed and drank from her pink cup, but it didn't taste like much.

And when Annemarie set Gerda in her doll chair she was not happy with her new life. From the overturned footstool at her feet, a short haired doll boy lifted his head with its large hole. Kurt, the no good, stuck out his tongue at her, as far as he could. Annemie had gone out of the room to drink her own cocoa.

The girl returned happily. Fräulein dressed her in a blue sailor jacket and white hat, ready for her walk. The Doll Mother put the Easter bunny cap with pink ears on Gerda's head.

"You look fine, my dear. We will to go to the zoo." Thereupon, Nesthäkchen threw Lolo out of her doll carriage, Baby wandering close behind. They ended up on the hard dolls' dresser. Annemarie did not see that Baby's knitted diaper panties were wet.

Gerda was placed in the white carriage. Annemarie carefully covered her with a pink silk blanket and put Irenchen's gorgeous red umbrella in her hand. On the stairs Gerda heard the indignant Irenchen's grumbles, which disturbed the joy of walking.

Doll mummy chattered and laughed continuously. She gave no thought to her poor neglected doll children at home.

She showed her new Gerda the wonders of Berlin: the porter at the doorstep, who was almost like the Emperor; the honking cars, the chocolate machine and the golden figure high on the Victory Column.

"Isn't it a fine world?" she asked her doll, face beaming.

Gerda forced a smile.

Oh yes, she would be pleased, if only the remaining dolls would not have been so ugly to her!

"Oh, Annemie, have you forgotten to set your other children in their garden on the flower board?" asked Fräulein when they returned home.

"Ah, they're old," was the indifferent reply, "I have a new, sweet Nesthäkchen."

Mommy entered the nursery.

"Think again, Lotte," she said earnestly, "what if I would not take care of Hans and Klaus, because of you, my Nesthäkchen. That would be sad for the two boys, right?"

The girl nodded and blushed. Then she reached silently toward her old dolls and put one after another on their garden-flower board, even Kurt, the rascal. But true love was missing.

In the afternoon, while Annemie and Gerda visited with Grandmother, a downpour pelted the poor dolls, who remained outside in the foul weather, and, moreover, without shelter. Frida closed the windows and brought the soggy dolls back into the nursery. Irenchen sneezed; she had caught a cold. Mariannchen shivered, Lolo got chills, Kurt complained of rheumatism, and Baby coughed.

Annemie, who heretofore had been such a good doll mother, didn't look at her sick children.

She had to prepare supper for her Nesthäkchen. She forgot Mommy's warning.

Gerda heard the sneezing and coughing, weeping, wailing and cursing of the poor dolls.

"We need to throw the new girl out of the house. Sneezy Sneezy! The brat! The rascal," grumbled Irenchen. "As soon as she put her nose here in the nursery, she stole Annemarie's love from us. We will tease her until she takes to her heels, the foreign shrimp, Sneezy Sneezy."

"I'll leave myself," Doll Gerda wanted to respond sadly, but Annemie pushed a bite of apple into her open mouth.

In the evening, as the two, Annemie and Gerda, lay together behind the white rails, the doll tossed restlessly back and forth. Annemie slept soundly, but poor Gerda did not.

Should she run away, so Annemarie could take care of her other children again? Oh, her mother had been so kind, so loving; the separation would break her heart.

The doll sobbed. Annemie moved.

"Why are you crying, my dear?" she asked in her dream.

"I must leave you again," wailed Gerda.

"What's the matter?" Annemarie asked, quite startled. "Was I bad to you? Was I sloppy with your stuff? Have I peeped too much?"

"Oh, no," whispered the doll in her ear, "You were good to me, too good! You have your other children, you must love them. Please forget all about me. You may be sad and scold me, but it's best if I go away." A tear rolled down Gerda's porcelain face.

"No, no, I will not let you go," Annemie cried in her dream and pressed her Nesthäkchen to her heart. "I prefer to be good again to my other dolls, Mommy has all her children. You must stay with me! "

Doll Gerda nodded and smiled through her tears.

And they both fell asleep.

Chapter 4.
We go to America--hooray!

Doll Gerda had been with her mom for two weeks. Day by day her situation pleased her more.

Annemarie kept the promise she made her doll in her dream: she became a good, loyal, caring mother to all her children. The dolls were full of gratitude, and they showed Gerda how they felt. They never revealed whether they had overheard the nocturnal conversation between the two, or whether Doll Gerda won their hearts with her modesty and kindness.

Peace returned to the nursery, and everyone was fond of the good Gerda. She could have been happy in her new home except for one member of the household. Puck completely terrified her. Puck was unaware that she suspiciously gazed at him from the side. Even when he licked her hand to manifest his friendly disposition, she looked anxiously to see if he had bitten her finger.

Brother Hans with his gaping fly bottle did not frighten Gerda. She was braver than that. Hans and Annemarie had recently caressed her amiably. Hans had made each of the two helmets from newspaper.

Oh, no, Gerda had no fear of Hans. But she did fear the boy whom the fly warned her about on the first morning: the eight-year old Klaus, the most dangerous person on earth.

Whenever he entered the nursery, the doll would have liked to crawl into the farthest corner, because he was always fighting and shouting.

Her initial contact was not promising. When Klaus saw the new doll, he welcomed her with a slap on the nose. He placed her on his sizable rocking horse and set it in such a furious gallop that the poor Gerda almost passed out. She would have been hurled from the saddle and her neck broken, if her mother Annemarie had not saved her with loud screams.

Another incident was much worse. The villain moved all his soldiers with their horses and guns to attack the doll baby.

"Fire!" he commanded with a general's voice that penetrated Doll Gerda to the bone. The guns thundered and the paper bullets whistled past the frightened doll child's head.

"I've been shot dead, stone dead," she cried and fainted.

In this piteous state Annemarie found her Nesthäkchen. Her kisses and tears brought the curly headed doll back to reality. The soldiers with their terrible cannons were marched off, but the war was not over. No, it raged on between Klaus and Annemarie. With clenched fists the girl defended her doll child until Fräulein joined them and transported the troublemaker Klaus from the nursery. But Gerda trembled as soon as she heard the voice of the wild boy from afar.

Frida cleaned the living room, and Annemarie helped. Of course Doll Gerda had to be there as well. She sat on the sofa like a lady and watched whether the two took care of her things.

Frida rubbed the windows clean, and the girl tapped the chair with her doll dust beater. Merrily the dust beater danced on the cushions, bum bum bum bum bum. What fun, especially because Gerda watched admiringly.

After a while Annemarie wanted to wash windows more than Frida did. The wet leather squeaked so melodiously on the panes.

"Please, Fridachen, we will exchange places. I will clean the windows and you can beat the furniture," suggested the girl.

"Hold on, Annemiechen, you will fall out of the window. It's two stories down. You will kill yourself," Frida said, frightened.

"The porter'd catch me. He's right below in the garden," said the girl.

"No, he is not there." Frida squeaked on with her leather.

"The good Lord would take care of me," Annemarie blathered.

"The good Lord has so much to do. He cannot watch out for every careless girl," Frida said, rubbing the window pane clean.

"The good Lord can see everything at the same time. Doesn't he have eyes in the back of his head, Gerda?" the girl exclaimed eagerly. The doll nodded yes, that was her view.

But Gerda agreed with Frida that Annemarie should not climb on the windowsill. She felt a hundred-pound-weight lift off her heart, as Frida suggested: "Annemiechen, would you rather clean the carpet with the carpet sweeper?"

Annemie lit up. The carpet sweeper squeaked more sonorously than the chamois leather. It needed oil. Rrrrrr it went on the blue carpet. The motor rumbled, creaked and whistled, cheering Annemie.

Rrrrrrr: ten times around in a circle, before the girl halted.

"Do you want a ride, Gerda?" she asked the expectant doll child.

Gerda held out both arms.

A second later, Gerda sat on the brown rattletrap.

"Now you're on the carousel, hold on tight, my darling," cried Annemie.

Gerda would have liked to tell her mom that it was not the merry go round, but she had enough to do. She held on tightly, so as not to be thrown off.

Rrrrrr: ten times around in circle before the carousel stopped.

"It was fine." Annemarie's and Gerda's eyes shined.

"Let's go to America, shall we, Gerdachen?"

The doll looked startled. She was afraid of seasickness.

"Ah, are you afraid to be alone on the ocean liner, you silly?" laughed her mother. "You wait, I'll keep you company." With that Annemarie was out the door. But it was not long before she reappeared, in one arm Irenchen and Mariannchen, in the other Lolo and Kurt, and in her bunched apron the kicking baby.

"So," she said, "the gentlemen want to travel to America, too. Please, take a seat, ladies. Gerda and Miss Irenchen go first class." She put the two on one side of the carpet sweeper and Lolo beside Mariannchen on the other, in second class. Irenchen, the oldest, got baby on her lap.

"I'm the captain and you, Kurt, are helmsman. Familiarize yourself with the mast of the ship." Annemie tied the doll boy with her blue hair ribbon to the brown wooden handle of the carpet sweeper.

"Do you have tickets, gentle- men? You can go on the journey. The blue carpet is the sea, or rather the great Ozehahn. I heard of it yesterday. Hans learned about it for his geography lesson," the captain said with dignity to her passengers.

"You mean *ocean,* not *Ozehan,*" warned Irenchen, who was in school and terribly clever. She could teach the Lord Cap- tain a thing or two.

The ship tooted "toot toot," the engine rumbled, squeaked and whistled, and the captain shouted: "We're going to Ameri- ca, hooray!"

The journey was through the middle of the blue sea. The proud ship rocked and swayed so much that one traveler tumbled over another.

"We go to America, hooray."

The captain fought bravely against storms and waves. Frida stood on the stepladder on shore, as if on a high lighthouse, and held her sides with laughter.

The passengers' hearts spun in their bodies on the dangerous journey. Gerda saw blackness before her eyes.

Mariannchen was cross and miserable. Irenchen looked even paler than usual; she was terribly sick. But the voyage progressed.

"We go to America, hooray."

"Man overboard!" cried Frida from her lighthouse. Horrified, Irenchen stretched her hands after Baby, who had fallen into the sea. Kurt, the courageous helmsman, jumped boldly after baby. The blue hair band, with which he had been tied, had slipped. But the captain let them both drown. That is part of a proper trip to America.

In the doorway appeared, attracted by the laughter and cheers, the curious Puck.

"Do you want to go to America, Puckchen? You must be my new helmsman." Before the dwarf pooch could bark "yes" or "no," the captain had assigned him to his new post and bound him to the mast.

"We go to America hooray!"

"Bow wow" snapped the angry new helmsman. It seemed to him extremely uncomfortable on the swaying ship.

Doll Gerda felt miserably seasick and had closed her eyes. She blinked anxiously toward the yelping helmsman.

"Dear God, I hope he does not bite me," she whispered.

Thump! The ship smashed into a reef, the bucket, and almost sank.

The unscrupulous helmsman left his post and escaped to the shore with a startled "bow wow." The passengers—Miss Gerda, Irenchen and Mariannchen, plunged headlong into the blue waters. Only Lolo traveled alone on the huge ship to America.

Hans and Klaus came home from school. When they saw their sister at her funny game, Hans suggested: "Come, Annemie, I'll make a ship of paper which you can tie in back as a lifeboat."

"Oh, Hänschen," cheered Annemarie and ran after her brother.

Klaus let his eyes sweep over the foundered ship's crew. Doll Gerda shivered in every limb, knowing the dangerous Klaus was in the room. Terrified, she felt his ink-smeared boyish hands on her arm, dragging her aloft.

"Heavens, he will finish me off," she thought with thumping heart.

Frida had left her ladder to fetch fresh water. Klaus, the rascal, climbed it with the poor doll. Higher and higher and higher they went.

"Does he want to carry me into the sky?" The doll, in her excitement, could scarcely grasp this idea.

Klaus halted. Wupp, Gerda sat half dead with fear, high up on the stove, which was heating the house during the cold days of April.

"Oh, I've burned myself," cried Gerda as the wild Klaus sneeringly slipped down the ladder.

Weeping, the doll remained enthroned on her hot lonely perch.

"Oh God, oh God, how will my mother find me here?"

Annemarie came radiantly back with her lifeboat. She tied it to the carpet sweeper and fished the drowned dolls out of the ocean.

"Hey, where has my Gerdachen gone?" she wondered. "Have you seen Gerda?" She turned to the other passengers.

Irenchen pointed with her outstretched arm in the direction of the furnace, but the girl paid no attention. Nor did she hear the fine, weeping doll voice which called her from above. Annemarie rushed into the boys' room. She knew at once the perpetrator.

Klaus sat there with the most innocent face in the world, doing his arithmetic homework.

"Klaus, did you take my Gerda?" She girded for battle.

"Let me alone about your stupid doll," he muttered and stuck his nose deeper into his book.

Nesthäkchen deemed it advisable to adopt another approach.

"Kläuschen, dear, good Kläuschen, ah, give me my little Gerda again!" She begged.

"You find her," growled the doll thief.

"So you've taken her, you vile boy. You'll get yours!" Annemarie prepared for fisticuffs with raised arms, but she lowered them and dashed out of the room. Her motherly love was a stronger impulse than her pugnacity.

"She swam to America, if she did not get swallowed by a shark," the naughty Klaus called out behind his sister.

In the living room Annemarie and Frida searched in every corner. Gerda was gone. The doll mother wept bitterly. On top of the stove her child wept equally bitterly.

Frida, cleaning the ceiling lamps, shouted from the ladder: "I see her. I see a leg over the edge of the oven. Hopefully she is not made of wax; otherwise she will have melted."

She moved the ladder to the furnace and rescued the poor doll child from being burned. Annemarie's heart beat well into her neck.

Dear God, would her Gerda, her sweet Nesthäkchen, be melted or darkened like Lolo?

She held her child in her arms, firmly, firmly. No, she was as beautiful as before but felt a bit warm. Blessedly she kissed Gerda, as though Gerda really had come from America.

From now on, Gerda had much, much greater fear of the evil Klaus.

Chapter 5.
Nesthäkchen makes bad weather

The trees in the Tiergarten park had grown their new, bright green May garments. The birdies chirped and whistled their spring songs, gorgeous lilacs flowered. In the trees ladybugs crawled; and on the playgrounds small boys and lasses romped.

The park was merry. Yet home was a thousand times merrier, and it was a fight for Annemarie to leave the house. The old, ugly winter dust was chased from every nook and cranny with large brooms, scrub brushes, and a veritable flood of soapy water. Hanne and Frida had it good. They did not have to walk with Fräulein in the ol' Tiergarten. They had the whole day to knock, brush, sweep, soap and mess to their heart's content. Oh, how Annemie envied them both, especially since Mommy often helped.

"Are you sad, Fräulein, that you can not pitch in?" Annemarie asked sympathetically, when they came to the park again.

"No, not at all," laughed Fräulein. "I'd much rather walk with you. How do you feel, Annemiechen?"

"Oh," cried the girl and laughed because she thought her Fräulein was kidding. She could not think that anyone would find something else more engaging than housecleaning. "I wish it rained every day. I would have to stay at home," she said fervently.

"That may come sooner than you think, darling, because the barometer is falling."

"Does it rain when the *barmeter* falls?" the girl asked earnestly.

"Yes, there is always bad weather," instructed Fräulein.

Today Annemarie was not quite on top of her game with regard to her thoughts. Gerda did not get to eat spinach, the ball remained in its red woolen net, and the large exercise rings did not pass as usual over her knees. Annemie had other things to do. She had to look into the blue sky and count the fluttering clouds that passed like white wool sheep. Would they bring rain?

When the girl came home from her walk, her first stop was not, as usual, the nursery to see her dolls. With hat and cloak she ran into Father's office, to the barometer. It clung firmly to the wall, an unhappy sign.

"Tomorrow we clean your nursery, my Lotte," Mom said after dinner to her daughter.

"Wonderful, since I cannot go for a walk." Annemarie joyously capered about, Gerda on her arm.

Mommy had a different view.

"You're not necessary, my dear heart. We cope well without you. On the contrary, it's even better if you do not stand in our way. "

"I must clean my doll kitchen myself. Hanne should not enter. She breaks my crockery. You said yesterday, Mommy, that Hanne smashes everything. "

"You can clean the doll kitchen yourself," said Mommy smiling. "Are you satisfied, Lotte?"

"No, no."

Nesthäkchen's face fell. "If my nursery is cleaned, I have to be there. In my nursery you must be well informed, Mommy. I must change and pat down my doll beds; oh, if it will only rain tomorrow."

Every few minutes Annemie ran to the window to look for black rain clouds. But the sky was blue and the sun laughed.

"You should not laugh at me, you stupid sun!" cried Annemarie and stuck out a smidgen of her red tongue. She quickly withdrew it. Doll Gerda looked at her Mama quite frightened.

But as the afternoon wore on and no rain clouds appeared, the girl took a bold decision: Annemie would make bad weather herself.

Heart knocking she crept with her Gerda into father's empty office.

Had Fräulein not said that when the barometer fell, it rained? Then it was certainly so because Fräulein knew everything.

The barometer hung on the wall.

On tiptoe the girl approached. Gerda made a fearful face.

The childish hand lightly touched the barometer, which annoyingly started to rock back and forth.

"Don't do it; let it alone," Doll Gerda wanted to warn; too late!

Annemie gave the Barometer a strong push. It swung, it bounced and it jumped frightened from its nail. Down it fell to the floor.

The glass broke in two, the pointers bent. Standing in front of the ruined instrument, the girl wept bitterly. Yes, there was a sudden rain, though only of Annemie's tears; outside the sun shone.

Shyly the small weather maker crept off.

After a while she heard the voice of Father when he returned home. He sounded upset.

"I want to know who ruined the expensive barometer, certainly during housecleaning." He was not nearly so shy as his daughter.

Mommy and Fräulein rushed in and looked startled at the destroyed barometer. They had no idea who could have committed the crime. Hanne and Frida were summoned, but protested their innocence.

"Send the boys to my room when they come out of gym class, Fräulein," Father angrily commanded. Annemarie could hear Father clearly. The doors were open. "I'm sure it was one of the rascals. They are in for some fun."

Twice Doll Gerda had plucked at the sleeve of Annemie's red muslin dress. She pretended not to notice. When the doll, for the third time, tugged more forcefully and looked at Annemarie reproachfully, the girl blurted: "Yes, I'm going."

And there she was with downcast eyes in father's office, her doll child pressed convulsively to the heart.

"Well, Lotte, what do you want?" Father said wrathfully when he saw his Nesthäkchen.

"Uh," she hemmed and hawed. She would have liked to run away, if she had not been ashamed before her doll child.

"What do you have on your mind, my Lotte?" Loving Father moved closer.

Annemarie wrapped her arms around Father's neck, and Doll Gerda did the same. Both hid their faces against his shoulder.

"I dropped the *Barmeter*," Annemarie whispered quietly.

"You?"

Father's face became serious. He pushed the sinner slightly away from him. "Why did you have to look at my barometer, Annemarie?"

"Annemarie" said Father, not "Lotte", as he usually did. He was not in a loving mood.

"I wanted rain tomorrow terribly. My nursery is being cleaned. Fräulein said if the *Barmeter* falls, there is bad weather," she sobbed in deepest pain.

"And therefore my silly Lotte dropped it?" Father bit his lips to hide his laughter.

Mom and Fräulein had to turn away their faces. They could not suppress their laughter.

Annemie didn't notice. She heard Father repeatedly call her "Lotte." Thankfully, he was no longer furious.

Doctor Braun took his youngest by the hand and pointed to the numbers which were printed on the barometer.

"See, Lotte, the bent blue and gold hands: they are terribly clever. They know perfectly well what kind of weather is ahead. If the weather is nice, they point to a higher number. If the weather is bad, they move to a lower number, and people say: The barometer falls. But no matter where the hands point, the barometer hangs quietly on the wall," said Father.

"Are you not angry, Daddy? I will never do it again," Annemie said shyly.

Father threatened with a smile: "Don't mess with my things anymore," and gave her a forgiving kiss. "Leave the future weather to our Dear Lord God, Lotte," he called after his happy daughter as she bounced away.

Doll Gerda felt the same. At night in her crib, Annemarie folded Doll Gerda's hands and her own and prayed, "Dear God, bring rain, hail and snow tomorrow. The *Barmeter* is kaput and can no longer do so. Amen!"

Chapter 6.
Lady bugs, flies...

The good Lord had heard Annemarie's prayer. There was no snow or hail the next day, but rain poured down in torrents and new rain clouds moved in.

No one was happier than Annemie. "Hurrah" she screamed and pressed her Gerda almost dead with bliss.

Mommy was less pleased. Her youngest was not to be lured from the nursery and was in everyone's way. With Annemarie involved, everybody would have her hands full.

Annemarie filled her small bucket with soda water and scoured her kitchen. The pretty brown paper, with which the floor was covered, could no longer be seen. She deluged the dollhouse and spoiled the pretty red plush carpet; she had forgotten to remove it. In the neatly swept nursery, a shower of semolina, rice, coffee, raisins and almonds rattled down; the miniature charwoman wanted the drawers of her merchant shop empty so that they could be washed out. Mommy pulled her daughter energetically out of the room. She was relegated to the next room, the boys' room, where her dolls had already migrated.

Doll Gerda beamed when she was in her mother's field of view. She was frightened to be left alone in the room of the dangerous Klaus, despite the fact that he was in school at the moment.

Annemie did not look at her children. She wailed: "Hanne can't finish up without me; she said it herself. Fridachen wants so terribly to keep me involved."

Mommy left the room. Annemarie turned to her doll children, and allowed them to comfort her in her pain.

Before long, she cautiously opened the door that led from the boy's room into the nursery. In the crack she shoved her tiny pug nose. Two blonde pigtails followed, and a moment later Nesthäkchen stood boldly and god-fearing on the threshold.

The nursery was beautiful beyond description. Wearing clogs, Hanne waded in a lake of soapy water and scrubbed the floor as Annemie before had the floor of her doll kitchen. This time the color did not depart with the dirt.

Carefully Annemarie put the outermost tip of her foot into the water. Ah, who needs to splash around in wooden clogs!

"You get your feet wet, and then you get sick; go back, Annemiechen" cried Frida.

The good Hanne saw Annemarie's longing glances. She dried her soapy hands on her apron and whoosh, there sat Nesthäkchen on the large, white nursery table, in the middle of the lake on an island.

She clapped her hands and slid back and forth with joy. Hanne was afraid that she could at any moment fly into the scrub bucket.

Mommy walked up and threatened the small intruder: "You wait, if you're not good, you'll be out of here, Lotte!"

Next door in the boys' room less joy reigned. In vain doll Gerda had held out her arms to her mother. She suspected that nothing good would come of Mom's frantic activity.

She was correct. Klaus came rumbling and whistling from school. He flung his satchel on the work desk and carefully placed a cigar box on the table. It buzzed and crawled with ladybugs he had captured in the Tiergarten.

He saw the doll family housed in his room. At the same time a thought shot through the rascal's head. He gently plucked one of the tingling beings from the box, took a long thread and tied it to the beetle's leg. The end of the thread he kept in his hand.

The beetle walked slowly over the oilcloth on the table. With anxious eyes the dolls watched him.

Gerda's heart thumped. She was not yet a year old and had never seen a beetle.

The brown stroller became aware of his freedom. He spread his wings as a test, counted to a hundred, and *burr,* he growled through the room to the window.

The dolls were in shock and almost fell on their backs. Gerda shook like a leaf, so scared was she of the brown beetle.

There was worse to come.

Klaus pulled the ladybug, buzzing against the window, back by his leash. Then he let him fly again.

Burr! This time the slender young beetle burred straight to the anxious dolls that had flocked to-gether. He liked young ladies. The dolls screamed in horror, and the beetle heard. The stupid Klaus did not understand the language of dolls.

The enterprising beetle was not disturbed by the defensively raised hands of young ladies. First he flew to the pale Irenchen who was blood red with fright, and tickled her nose. Then he burred toward Mariannchen's glued eyes; finally he sat on Gerda's blond curls and tenderly crawled on her face. She was indeed the most beautiful thing.

Gerda did not appreciate the caresses.

"Help" she cried, "Help," and fell into a dead faint.

Klaus pulled her brown cavalier by the looped thread around his leg back into his dungeon.

Puck gave the dangerous Klaus a wide berth today; as soon as he saw the cigar box, he knew what hour the bell had struck.

It was inexplicable to Puck that smart people called May the merry month. He detested May outright. During no other month did ladybugs shoo him so avidly from his rest. Klaus set the tingling things on his cold, black dog's snout, then on his long white silky coat. The dwarf pooch snapped, barking at the naughty beetles tormenting him. The nasty Klaus did not interfere. And Hans, who otherwise harmlessly went his own way, got ladybug mania and teased the dog. No, Puck had no enthusiasm at all for the merry month.

Most afraid of the brown beasts, more than all the dolls and Puck, was Nesthäkchen. She screamed when Klaus showed her his foreboding cigar box from a distance. Then she stormed to Fräulein for help putting on her long stockings. She knew well that Klaus aimed to stick beetles into her knee length socks.

Annemie dared not enter the boys' room. She remained all day under Mum's and Fräulein's protection. The poor Gerda had to recover from her faint alone.

That evening, the nursery was ready. It flashed with cleanliness. New white muslin curtains shone on the windows. All the beds, even the dolls', were white and crisp.

The evil Klaus crept with his ladybug box secretly into the nursery.

Just under the bed of his little sister he put the box. As a precaution, he left the lid a bit open, so that the prisoners were not stifled.

It was the middle of the night. Everyone was asleep in the nursery. It began to rain in the cigar box. One after another of the brown fellows marched through the air gaps to freedom, and burr! The whole swarm burred onto the new white muslin curtains.

Burr! they went, merrily through the nursery. Four flew to Annemie's crib, three to Fräulein, and half a dozen burred around the doll carriage, tingling and crawling.

Annemie's nose itched in her sleep. A beetle grandpa had landed on it. Fräulein ran her hands about in the air; she had a beetle between her fingers. Doll Gerda tore at her frightened eyes when she heard the terrible burring and whirring, and her crying awoke her little Mama. Amidst the burring Annemarie recognized the voice of her doll.

"Fräulein, Fräulein, an airship must be in the room. Listen to it hum," she shouted.

Fräulein turned on the light. Shocked, she saw the captured beetle in her hand and beetles wherever she looked.

The crib was surrounded by funny burring ladybugs. They nestled next to Gerda who screamed as though she had been stabbed.

Fräulein lovingly calmed her small, roaring Annemie. Then she opened both windows and burr! The entire company flew out, never to return.

The nursery, which had just been cleaned, looked funny the next morning. The beautiful white muslin curtains were black. Black spots covered the freshly made beds. The beetles had made the room dirty again.

Klaus got his well deserved wallops.

Chapter 7.
"Doctor, my child is so sick!"

On the playground one day were three cute kids, a boy and two girls. Annemie looked at them from a distance, pushing her doll carriage closer and closer. One of the strange children asked: "Child, do you want to play with me," and began to cough. The girl coughed until she was lobster red in the face. She could not stop coughing. Then the other two began to cough. Annemie pitied the three; she had never heard someone coughing so much.

They were walking around barefoot. Their mom had forbidden it, and God had sent them the nasty cough as punishment.

Before Annemarie could inquire, Fräulein stood behind her and pulled her back with a scared face. She grabbed her handiwork from the bench, tied on Annemarie's gray play apron, and sat her red southwester hat on her little blond head.

With immense astonishment Annemarie watched. As Fräulein took her hand and turned to leave the playground, Annemarie reacted.

"My doll carriage, my Gerda," she cried and tried to break away from Fräulein's hand to retrieve her forgotten doll carriage from the strange children. But Fräulein did not let her continue.

"You wait for me here, Annemie; I'll get the doll carriage."

Annemie's amazement grew. Gerda made big eyes, like never before. Fräulein rolled the doll carriage herself.

When the little girl laughed brightly over the comical sight, Fräulein looked so serious that Annemie, alarmed, fell silent. Had she been naughty?

Annemie drew her brow together and thought hard. She could not remember any misbehavior, despite her best effort.

"Fräulein," she began shyly after she had walked silently beside her, "I know I was bad. I won't be bad again, ever!"

"What, Annemiechen?" It was Fräulein's turn to make a surprised face.

"Wasn't I naughty?" asked Annemarie doubtfully. "Why are you mad? Why are you taking me home?"

"I'm not angry, sweetheart, but I am anxious that you might be infected. We're not going home, only to another part of the park. On the playground the children had whooping cough." Fräulein said the last words with a worried face.[1]

---

[1] Vaccination has virtually eliminated whooping cough as a childhood disease, but in 1909 it ranked first among acute infections as a cause of

Whooping cough: Mom had warned her children about it. Annemie secretly wished many times to see what Mom was talking about.

"They have certainly not infected me, Fräulein, I was dressed so warmly. I'm coughing a bit. But why shouldn't I push my doll carriage myself?"

"You can't touch Gerda or the doll carriage today. We need to thoroughly clean them both, so you do not infect yourself."

"My Gerda? Has she got whooping cough?" Nesthäkchen looked at her doll closely. But Gerda didn't cough once. Annemarie seemed surprised at Fräulein's precautions.

On reaching home, Doll Gerda was more curious. Her little mama did not take her out to play. Instead, Gerda was placed on the middle of the balcony in the sun. There she sat all day long, and had no other society than the boring doll carriage. But when it got dark, and Annemarie did not come to remove her Gerda and take her to bed, the doll was angry with her doll mother. She was a healthy doll, but in the night air she would catch a cold.

---

death in children, exceeding diphtheria and scarlet fever in gross mortality. Whooping cough is highly infectious and occurred in frightening epidemics.

Oh, Doll Gerda did not know that her little Mama feared exactly the same fate and implored Fräulein to be allowed to bring Gerda inside.

Mom and Fräulein insisted that Gerda should sleep in the open tonight. Father, who rarely rejected an appeal from his Nesthäkchen, said: "In all cases it is better."

The next day Annemie was allowed to bring her child inside. Fräulein had dressed the doll in different clothes and sprinkled Gerda with a vile perfume.

"Pooh, Gerda, you smell like father's office!" Beaming Annemie wanted to hold her favorite doll in her arms. But as she got close, she sniffed and turned away her head.

Doll Gerda was resentful. She could certainly not help being perfumed with the vile stuff. Lysol, Fräulein had called it. She turned her curly head to one side and did not look at her little Mama.

For the first time in their lives, the two were angry with one another. Annemarie took Irenchen to the park, and Doll Gerda sat stiff and silent on her doll chair, as though Annemarie were the air she breathed.

Annemie was sad that evening and said, "I would like to take Gerda to bed, if she didn't smell so horrible." The doll thought defiantly: "I'll never, ever sleep with you again; I want nothing to do with you, you old Annemarie."

Both wept themselves to sleep, the girl in her crib and the doll on her stool.

Next day the two were still angry with each other. But on the third morning, although Gerda wanted to make no friendly face, her mom took her on her lap.

"Have you anything to say to me, Gerda?" she asked her Nesthäkchen, quite like Mom when Annemarie had been rude.

Gerda was silently obdurate. She did not respond.

Annemarie herself did not have an entirely clear conscience. She gave her doll child a make-up kiss. The Lysol smell was gone.

Gerda was obstinate; she went rigid and did not want to be kissed.

"Fräulein, I do not know what to do with the naughty child, she is so terribly stubborn," said the doll mother perplexed as she placed Gerda in the corner.

"Maybe she's sick," said Fräulein soothingly.

"Sick yes, it's possible, whooping cough."

Gerda was brought out from her sofa corner. The doctor's daughter felt her pulse and put her bath thermometer under the doll's left arm, to see if she had a fever.

"Fräulein, it reads seventy-six degrees, the child has a terribly high fever. She must immediately go to bed!" Before Gerda knew what was happening, she was undressed and lying in bed by Irenchen and Mariannchen. Yet she felt completely healthy.

Most unpleasantly, her Annemie laid a dripping washcloth like a cold compress on her forehead. Oh, she should have been naughty and refused it.

Annemie found that Gerda's fever rose. The bath thermometer indicated ninety degrees. The worried mother sent her doll boy Kurt to Doctor Puck.

He lay on the sofa, where he was not allowed, and was taking a nap. He planned to look after the dolls later.

Gerda was shocked when the curtain was pushed back on her four-poster bed. The white-bearded face of Doctor Puck appeared.

"I'm not sick, I'm quite well," she called, but no one listened to her.

Doctor Puck put his cold paw on her forehead, looked at her intently and then said with a shrug, "Bow wow." That meant in German: "I do not know what's wrong with your doll."

Annemie decided to consult a famous doctor for advice, so Gerdachen would not die.

It was after office hours. The patients were gone. There was a knock on the door of Doctor Braun's modest consulting room.

The doctor got up and opened the door. Had he forgotten a patient?

Before him stood a little lady with a jacket, which had a long train. On her head she wore an elegant plumed hat. To Doctor Braun she seemed familiar, especially the two tiny pigtails peeking out. In her arm she held something long, wrapped in a large cloth.

"Good day, sir, my child is so sick!" said the little lady with a disguised voice and worried face.

"Oh, sorry, come nearer, madam, please sit down," said Doctor Brown, directing the patient to a chair.

Blessedly Annemie seated herself. She was the little lady with Mum's plumed hat.

"Bring the child over here, ma'am," commanded the doctor.

The large cloth was opened and Gerda appeared.

"Well, my dear, what's wrong?" asked the friendly doctor. Gerda was not nearly as afraid of him as she was of Doctor Puck.

"I think the child has whooping cough," the small Mom said.

"She coughs that much?"

"No, not at all, but she has ninety-nine degrees of fever."

"Well, then I'll see that your daughter quickly recovers, madam," said the famous physician.

He pulled out his black stethoscope, laid it on Doll Gerda's chest, and put his ear to the earpiece. Then he tapped Gerda's chest, while Annemie thought proudly: "Father examines more extensively than Puck."

The doctor said reassuringly: "The little one seems to have caught a cold."

"Not whooping cough?" The mother seemed not quite satisfied.

"No, she has little glands. I'll make her a bandage. Tomorrow she is back to full health." Dr. Braun took bandages and made doll Gerda such an intricate conglomeration that she could not move her head.

With reverent eyes her little Mama watched. She envied her child the elegant bandage.

"So, madam, the patient is taken care of."

"Madam" did not stand up. She looked at the doctor with begging eyes.

"Would you like anything else, madam?"

"I would so like to have the same bandage." A wistful sigh emerged from the lips of the young lady.

"You, Ma'am?" The famous doctor looked strangely merry. "You are quite healthy. Is anything wrong? "

"My two thumbs hurt me so, that may be my problem." The little lady worried about pneumonia. She pointed to the famous doctor with her thumbs, which were inky but quite healthy.

"I will give you a prescription, madam: wash carefully with soap," ordered the doctor.

Annemie disagreed. She wanted to have her bandage. She needed it worse than Gerda.

Madam said amiably "adieu, Herr Doktor," but forgot to thank him.

The door was not closed long behind the patient, when Doctor Braun heard a piercing scream.

Frightened, he ran after his daughter.

In the living room was the little lady with the beautiful plumed hat. In her right hand she held a pair of scissors, while she held out her left with pitiful cries, "Oh oh, it bleeds" and a moment later, smiling painfully: "I must have a bandage."

"You stupid little Lotte," said Dr. Braun, foregoing all respect. "How did you get to the scissors? You should not touch them."

"I wanted so terribly to have a proper bandage, and because my thumbs were so frightfully healthy, I needed a tiny cut. But the ol' scissors made a big cut. Oh oh, it does hurt so much."

"Lotte, this is your punishment. You have handled the scissors and cut yourself willingly. Now you must endure the pain," father said gravely. But he took his weeping Nesthäkchen into the consulting room and made her a dressing which was much nicer than Gerda's.

Oh, how proud Annemie was. Now she didn't hurt as much.

The next day doll Gerda could dispense with her bandage. She was cured. Her small mom had to go several more days with a bandaged hand.

Neither got whooping cough.

Chapter 8.
Barrel Organ

Annemarie sat with her children in their garden outside on the flower board. Iron bars had been fitted so that she could not fall out the window. Annemie had sown lovely flowers in her garden: morning glories, beans and watercress. Unfortunately, she could not tell for the time being. Not the smallest green shoot wanted to show itself in the cigar boxes filled with brown earth, because Annemie dug them up daily, to see if they had begun to sprout green leaflets.

The dolls liked their garden. The sun shone brightly and warmly. Irenchen's pale cheeks began to redden softly. Antics, whose summer residence was on the flower board, fluttered and sang merrily; black and gray sparrows perched on the roof devoutly listening.

Oh, you could see everything. Doll Gerda stretched her neck. And her curious Mama did the same.

Over at the Müllers, Auguste was ironing at the open window. A floor lower, in the home of the privy counsel, the fat cook stirred food and sang almost as nicely as Antics. Opposite in the nursery, Annemie's friend, little Rolf, who recently had been sick and looked paler than Irenchen, longingly pressed his nose against the windowpane. The poor guy could not run out.

How he would have loved to be sitting with Annemie and her dolls on the flower board!

Annemie nodded a greeting to her friend, and all the dolls nodded, too. Then they saw something more enchanting.

In the courtyard, the porter turned on for the first time today the small fountain that stood in the middle of the round lawn. A small stone statue of a naked infant spurted water happily from his mouth. Annemie believed he was rinsing his mouth, and the dolls thought the same. Gerda wondered why the cherub brushed his teeth in the middle of the courtyard. Why wasn't he wearing a camisole or night skirt? Why wasn't he properly dressed?

At the fountain, every porter's child had gathered, joined by some neighborhood friends. It was an event when the fountain was turned on. Annemie looked up from her airy seat full of admiration for the porter, who accomplished this miracle. She was certain that she wanted to be a porter.

It was good that the flower board window had bars; otherwise Annemie would already have plopped into the yard. The curious girl kneeled on the flower board to get a better look, and poked her pug nose through the iron bars. The dolls sat up against the bars. In the courtyard it was gorgeous.

Karle, the bandy-legged porter's boy, let a paper boat float into the sea of the spring well. Paule, his brother, whipped round about, hopping from one corner of the courtyard to the other. Amanda raced along on roller skates that sounded like an express train. The other children stood watching the black Grete, the garrulous magpie, who lived in a cage in the porter's lodge and proudly pretended she herself was the porter. When anyone entered the house, she called politely in a croaking voice, "What do you want, sir?" and a moment later less politely: "Stop thief! Halt thief!"

Oh, who wouldn't like to be down there? But Mommy did not allow her youngest to play in the yard, although it was a thousand times jollier than the park.

The small courtyard company became lively. Their interest in the black Grete disappeared. All the blue, gray and brown children's eyes turned with blissful gleam on a rather ragged old man who had set foot in the courtyard. On his back he carried a large box, and in his hand a wooden frame.

"The organ grinder, the organ grinder," sounded jubilantly from the window.

Annemie clapped her hands for joy. The cooks opened their kitchen windows and looked out.

The organ grinder set up his stand, put the box on it, turned the crank of the barrel organ, and the concert began.

A happy waltz: the children in the courtyard entwined in pairs and started dancing. The fat cook at the window swayed her hips. Auguste and her iron danced over the laundry. The pale Rolf drummed on the window, and the black Grete beat time with her wings. Annemie turned to her dolls, amidst the beautiful music, and thought fervently: "Oh, if I were not Annemie Braun. If I were a porter's child, I could dance along down there."

As the organ grinder ended his performance, paper wrapped coins flew down from many windows. He gathered up the money gratefully. The children helped.

Annemie ran to Mommy, who was with Fräulein storing winter clothes to protect them from moths. The abominable smell of camphor and pepper crawled in the girl's nose.

"Sneezy Sneezy," sneezed Nesthäkchen. "Mom, oh, please, give me a six for the organ grinder. Achoo! Achoo!"

Mommy laughed at her daughter's sneezing and gave Nesthäkchen the desired coin.

Eagerly the girl ran back to her garden. She wrapped the money in newspaper as you have never seen it. The packet whizzed through the air and landed on the head of the stone fountain cherub. Hops, the journey continued into the fountain water with a splash.

"My money, my money is drowning!" shouted Annemie to the barrel organ polka sounds.

The bowlegged dancing porter's boy Karle heard the girl, fished the money from the shallow lake and gave it to the organ grinder.

"Thanks, little lady!" cried the organ grinder, tipping his battered hat. Then he played a fine gallop.

Hoopla! Like goats on the farm the kids jumped among one another. Hoopla! Above, the doll kids hopped, much more boisterously.

Gerda galloped with Kurt along the board among the wild flowers. She exclaimed: "My shoe, my gold bug shoe!"

Gerda and Annemarie peered down frightened through the iron bars. They saw a small, golden brown object land on the grass.

Perplexed, the two looked at each other.

Annemie found her tongue first.

"That's what happens, Gerda, if one is so wild! Now you can figure out how to get back your pretty shoe. The organ grinder will think it's money and throw it in his box," said the doll's Mama.

The doll made a contrite face and twitched her mouth tearfully.

Annemie felt sorry for her Nesthäkchen. She took Gerda in her arms and said, "Come, let us ask Hanne to bring you back your shoe."

But the kitchen was empty, Hanne had gone shopping. Frida was nowhere to be seen.

Annemarie pondered hesitantly for a moment, then stood at the kitchen door and whoosh!

She was holding her Gerda as she ran down the back stairs.

Her heart was beating so loudly that Gerda could hear it. The girl was well aware that she was doing something forbidden. She quieted the voice of her conscience, which warned her to turn back: "Oh, I'll be right back up, Fräulein. The moths won't notice."

When Annemie arrived in the yard among the enthusiastic children, she no longer listened to the warning voice in her head.

The jolly dancing below was a thousand times more fun than it had looked from the flower board.

Gerda had her golden shoe back and would have liked to run upstairs quickly, but her small mom did not want to leave. Annemarie cried out as she was spattered with water from the cherub in the fountain. Gerda got a good shower, too.

Annemarie turned to the bowlegged Karle and danced the Polka. Then she danced a two-step with Paule. Doctor's Nesthäkchen hopped with bare legs and high spirits among the other kids.

Amanda had taken Gerda in her arms and stroked her, admiring her fine dress. All the other girls stood around and looked enviously at the beautiful doll's curls. Gerda was not pleased at the admiration of strange children. Annemie had been bad but no longer thought of returning to the house. Gerda bore the blame. Her lost gold shoe had caused Annemarie to run away. Heavens, they both would soon be missed upstairs.

The organ grinder had meanwhile strapped his organ to his chest and moved to the next house. The children ran along behind.

Annemie talked to the black Grete and wanted to die laughing. The bird called her "sir."

The girl pondered a moment. She took her Gerda by the hand and followed behind the strange children, although Gerda by no means wanted to.

The naughty child thought nothing of Mommy's interdiction, nor of Mom's fear and anxiety. Annemie thought solely of the organ grinder.

Meanwhile Fräulein entered the nursery and said, "Annemiechen, I'm done, we can get dressed and go for a walk."

But no Annemie sat on the flower board.

Certainly the goblin had hidden somewhere, and Fräulein looked for her. But she was not under the bed, behind the game cabinet, or behind the wardrobe curtain, her favorite hiding place.

Annemie had to be found. Fräulein had never cried so loudly. "Annemiechen, child, it's getting late." No Annemie appeared.

Fräulein's heart began to beat with fear. From the flower board the child could not fall. The window was barred.

The yard was empty. Only the black Grete sat there in the sunshine.

Had Fräulein merely asked the dolls about Annemarie; they knew where their doll mother was. Fräulein did not ask them.

Fräulein ran distraught to Mother and said, "Ma'am, our Annemie's gone."

Mom was pale with fright, but then said, reassuring herself: "Oh, Fräulein, the child must be with the girls."

"The girls have both gone to the laundry." Nevertheless, Fräulein chased into the kitchen, the anxious Mrs. Braun in hot pursuit.

They found the open kitchen door.

It was clear that Annemie had run away!

"I'm going straight to the police. My Nesthäkchen, my Lotte, where are you?" wailed Mother, who already had her hat on.

"Maybe the doorman saw her when she walked down the back stairs. We want to ask him, at any rate," advised Fräulein. Both women rushed down the back stairs.

The doorman had seen many children in the yard. He was not sure if Doctor's Nesthäkchen had been there.

Mom, in her anxiety, was ready to run to the police. Hanne and Frida with their laundry basket entered the courtyard. And who accompanied them, with hot cheeks and shining eyes? the grinning Nesthäkchen with her Gerda, whom Hanne and Frida had picked up off the street and brought home.

Mom, Mommy, it was fine; we danced to the organ grinder. I can do the two step," the girl called sweetly, without a glance at Mum's and Fräulein's worried faces.

Mommy took her daughter's hand tightly, as if she was afraid that she might escape her again, and said, with a face that did not bode well: "We'll have further words upstairs."

Oh, there would be a serious conversation between Mom and her youngest, and the rod behind the mirror would also have a few words to say. The rod would show that it could dance as beautifully as Annemie. Worst was that her child, her Gerda, was ashamed to look at her.

The runaway girl was not allowed to come to lunch at noon. She had to eat in her room with Gerda. Both would be ashamed before father and the boys.

Annemie was mortified in front of black Grete. As soon as the bird saw her, she exclaimed, in a voice that echoed through the house: "Stop thief! Stop thief!"

Chapter 9
"Tomorrow we sweep!"

It was late. Annemie had already put her children to bed. It was high time for her to go to sleep as well.

The moon was in the sky. But the girl didn't care. First she wanted to pray with Irenchen, then lubricate Mariannchen's eyes with ointment.

She had forgotten to give a goodnight kiss to her Gerda.

"Annemie, if you are not good and do not quickly go to bed, tomorrow we don't go to the place in the park where the children play so joyfully," threatened Fräulein. That helped. Annemie's ardent desire, with which she tormented Fräulein for days, was to be allowed to participate in the games of the merrily singing children.

"I must say goodnight to Mum, Fräulein. I'll be right back."

On the threshold of the living room, which she had to pass through to get to the dining room, the girl stopped undecided.

It was so dark, so terribly dark, the silly girl was afraid.

"Fräulein," she cried, running back, "dear, good, only Fräulein, please come with me."

"Why?" said Fräulein. "Must you have a travel companion from here to the dining room?"

"No but," said the girl, ashamed of her foolish fear.

"Go to bed," said Fräulein, who knew the weaknesses of the girl and had already taken the hair bands off her pigtails.

"No, that will not do," ranted Nesthäkchen, "when I haven't said goodnight to Mom, I can't fall asleep, can I, Gerda?" Annemie went to her crib. But Gerda's eyes were firmly closed and the doll no longer answered.

"Please, dear, all best Fräulein, come with me," the cuddly kitten begged. She climbed up on the chair, threw her arms around Fräulein's neck, and nuzzled her sweet face into Fräulein's cheek.

It was difficult indeed to refuse Annemarie anything.

"Tell me, at least, why you don't want to go alone," demanded Fräulein.

"It's so terribly dark in the living room and I become mad with fear," confessed the terrified bunny.

"You are afraid, yes, but of whom?"

"Klaus could hide and play Red Riding Hood's Wolf. He jumps from behind a chair and frightens me."

Fräulein opened the door to the boys' room.

"Klaus is sitting in his room politely at his supper. He does not think of scaring you. Go quietly, Annemie, show that you are a grownup, sensible girl."

But Annemie did not want to be grownup and sensible. Fräulein had better come with her.

"A black man is in the living room," the girl whispered shyly, hiding her face behind her hands.

"Annemie!" Fräulein was angry. "How do you come by such nonsense? There is no black man!"

"No, just brown," said Nesthäkchen.

"Absolutely not, you silly, where did you hear this folderol?"

"Frida told me the other evening when you were in the theater, Fräulein. I could not fall asleep. I tossed and turned with Gerda. Frida threatened me: 'The black man comes. He will be in the living room,' she said."

"That's wrong of Frida to tell you something like that, but, Annemie, it is equally wrong to believe such applesauce. You know that God is with you everywhere to protect you. "

"Yes, but maybe he is asleep at night."

"The good Lord never sleeps. He shelters people during the night, Luv."

"Does the sandman come to dear God?"

"No, child." Fräulein smiled.

"I want to be dear God and never have to go to my ol' bed at night," said Nesthäkchen with a deep sigh.

She forced Fräulein to kindle a light in order to prove to the silly thing that nothing fearful, absolutely nothing, was in the living room.

Annemie received her goodnight kiss from Mom and lay in her bed. She was awfully glad she was not dear God watching out all night for so many, many people. She was tired and her eyes closed quickly.

The next day Fräulein went with Nesthäkchen to the playground as promised. After she had convinced herself that no one coughed suspiciously, she gave Annemarie permission to play with other children.

"Will you ask if they want to play me, Fräulein," she said shyly.

"No, child, you have a mouth. If you want to play along, you need only ask."

"I'm shy," whispered Annemie and bowed her blond head almost to the ground.

"You need not be embarrassed," Fräulein said, "Dive right in, Luv."

Annemie could not decide. She stood with her Gerda close to the circle of playing children, and both of them made longing eyes. The children sang, "A farmer went into the wood." Oh, how gladly the two would have been potted plants, or at least servant and whip.

But when the children sang, "Do you want to know how the farmer," which Annemie thought was so melodic, she overcame her shyness.

"You, may I play?" Blushing, she asked a child who was near.

But he sang instead of answering, with blaring voice. "See so, so, goes the farmer, beware, so, so, goes the farmer, beware, so, so, moves the farmer his sheaves from the field." The children ran around in circles like harvest wagons. They almost trampled the eager Annemarie.

"Ouch!" she cried, rubbing her stomped feet. She was stomped again and began to cry. But she did not cry out in pain, because she would not be allowed to play.

A larger girl became aware of the crying thing.

"Come on, do not cry, little one," she said consolingly, "Play with us." She took Annemie by the hand.

Beaming, tears trickling down her cheeks, Annemarie was blissful. With her right hand she touched the nice girl, with her left doll Gerda, who in turn gave her hand to a boy who was as thick as he was tall.

So the circle of children danced around while they sang: "If we go to the lake, where the little fish swim ..."

Annemarie was a goldfish, and Gerda was a squid. But should the squid follow the other fish and grasp the back of the dress in front of her? Gerda was too stupid. Annemie took the doll in her arms and said apologetically: "The little one is not a year old, she is my Nesthäkchen."

And when the sad story of "Little Mary sat on a stone," was acted out, the stupid Gerda was afraid that she was to be shot to death together with Little Mary. She was glad that her mamma introduced the dangerous game "Cat and Mouse," and she could safely join Fräulein.

Gerda saw how happily the children played "Long, long linen," "Bird Sale," and "Pull through, pull through the golden bridge." Gerda would have been happy to be pulled through the golden bridge. But her doll mother seemed to have completely forgotten her. Annemarie was no longer shy. She cheered and whooped the loudest.

Suddenly Annemie appeared next to Fräulein and Gerda on the bench. She made a frightened face and no longer wanted to play.

"Have you quarreled with someone?" asked Fräulein uneasily.

"Oh no," protested Annemie, "I'm overheated." She took out her handkerchief. She waved her hand to cool herself.

Jubilant children's voices cried out: "Who's afraid of the black man?"

"Not for a penny."

Fräulein knew what was wrong.

"Oh, Annemie," she said meaningfully, "Are you so afraid of the black man that you do not want to play?"

The girl stood in silent embarrassment. Doll Gerda was highly disrespectful: "My Mama is ten times more stupid than I!"

"You know that there is no black man, Annemie," said Fräulein.

"Why are the dumb kids saying it if he doesn't exist?" said the girl uncomfortably.

"It's a game, dear heart. There's no golden bridge. There's no linen that has legs and runs away by itself. Play along quietly, then you will see how pretty the game is, and that my little silly need not be afraid."

Annemie hesitated. The cheers of the children increased as she turned around. Annemarie sought protection with doll Gerda.

Soon the voice of Doctor Braun's Nesthäkchen was the boldest in the children's chorus: "Not for a red cent." No, Annemie was not afraid now, "not for a red cent," of the black man. Neither was Gerda.

The park had never been as fine as it was today. But everything comes to an end, including a morning. One child after another said goodbye. Annemie shook hands and promised to come back tomorrow.

"Is it not true, Fräulein, we come back tomorrow?" she asked on the way home.

"Of course, if you are well behaved today," promised Fräulein.

Annemie made every effort to behave in an exemplary manner, because she wanted the pleasure of playing with the children in the park.

That afternoon, when Fräulein wrote a birthday letter to her mother, Annemie politely went into her nursery, in order not to disturb her. Annemarie was also mannerly in Hanne's kitchen. All the dolls followed their Mama's example and made no noise, even the wild Kurt.

"Rejoice, Hanne, that we pay you a short visit," said Nesthäkchen, and made her entry into the kitchen with the dolls.

"OK." Red faced Hanne laughed and rubbed her pots.

Hanne looked up after a while, because Annemie seemed well behaved. It was downright scary. In the quiet room Hanne no longer laughed.

Gosh, what happened to her nice clean kitchen?

The small visitors poured sand from the sandpit on the tiles and children sat in it. With a spoon and a small pot they baked cake to their hearts' content.

"We are here in the Tiergarten, Hanne, on the sand play-ground," Annemarie said quickly when she saw the horrified face of the cook. Would Hanne scold her?

No, to the good Hanne Nesthäkchen was too dear. Hanne could not be angry with her. She swept the scattered sand together and said, "You know what, Annemiechen, play something else."

The girl was in agreement. Today she wanted to behave in an exemplary manner. She was thankful to Hanne that she had not rebuked her. The dolls knew all the wonderful games that Annemie had played in the park, and were to make a presentation.

Unfortunately, the dolls acted quite silly. They bickered with each other. Kurt didn't like to touch Irenchen. Lolo wanted to put Mariechen to work combing her black hair. Mariannchen tripped over her own feet and ended up with a bump on her forehead. Annemie made short work of the situation and placed the dolls as spectators on the kitchen cupboard. Only Gerda was allowed to give a presentation.

"Hanne, are you afraid of the black man?" asked Nesthäkchen as a precaution before they began the beautiful game.

"God forbid," chuckled Hanne.

"Well, we are not either, is that not so, Gerdachen?"

With a ringing voice that set all the pots shaking, Annemarie shouted:" Who is afraid of the black man?"

"Not for a red cent."

The doorbell rang at the back door.

In her enthusiastic singing, the girl had not heard it. When Hanne opened the door, Nesthäkchen approached, curious.

"Ooh, the black man" With spine tingling fright the girl crept into the far corner.

Yes, there he stood, the black man, a ladder on his shoulder and a broom in his hand.

"Tomorrow I'll sweep," he cried with a loud voice. But when he saw the fear of the silly girl, he smiled. White teeth flashed in his black face.

"You're not scared of me, are you, little one?" he asked amiably.

Annemie, who had boldly sung "not for a red cent," hid her trembling face behind her apron.

"You silly, he's the chimney sweep," reassured the good Hanne.

Annemie took the apron from her face. She squinted sus-piciously at the black man.

The dolls sat on the kitchen cabinet and laughed uproari-ously at their silly mummy.

Chapter 10.
The Chocolate Marshmallow Moorkop Pastry

"We have a visitor. Aunt Albertina comes today." Jubilantly Annemie danced around the room.

Aunt Albertina was an old lady who could rarely make the long journey. But Annemie rejoiced every time she came to visit.

First, Auntie always had something sweet for Nesthäkchen in her voluminous handbag. Second, the girl could come into the dining room, say "Good day," and stay for a while because she was Aunt Albertinchen's favorite. Third and most important, there was habitually cake and whipped cream.

Today Nesthäkchen examined the coffee table before Aunt arrived. Mmmm, the large moorkop chocolate cream pastry next to the magnificent marzipan potato: of all pastries these two were Annemarie's favorites. She could taste the tempting confections in her little belly. If she were the old aunt she could choose something delectable from the cake bowl.

"Mom, do we get cake today?" she asked expectantly.

"If Aunt Albertina leaves us some," smiled Mommy.

"Oh, she can not eat it all alone. Old ladies have weak stomachs. She'll be sick tomorrow," prophesied Nesthäkchen philanthropically.

However, Aunt Albertina lived a long way off. Waiting for her could stimulate the appetite.

"Mommy," said the thoughtful girl, "you could stick a piece of paper with my name on the moorkop or the marzipan potato, or perhaps both, so that Aunt Albertina knows that they are intended for me."

"But they are not meant for you, Lotte, but for Auntie," laughed Mommy.

Annemie had to temper her aspirations. She ran into the nursery, went to the window, looked piously up at the blue sky and clasped her hands: "Dear God," she prayed, "You see everything and can do anything. Concern yourself, please, with the fact that Aunt Albertina should only take crumb cake and pretzels. She must leave some of the moorkop and the beautiful marzipan potato for me. Amen."

Tranquilized, Annemie went to her dolls. Gerda had to be spruced up. She should come and welcome Auntie, who had not seen her. She would certainly be pleased to make Gerda's acquaintance.

"Do not be cheeky, Gerda, only respond when Aunt asks you something. You do not need to be shy and embarrassed, or to hide yourself. Wear your pretty pinafore. I have flattened it with my iron. And don't squint at the cake dish. You look like a terrible glutton, do you hear, Gerda?" Thus Annemie exhorted her child for her first social appearance.

Gerda nodded assent to everything. She would behave in a ladylike manner.

Her mummy was dressed to the nines. But Annemarie's face was perpetually ink-smeared. Where she got dirty hands was a complete mystery to Fräulein. Her blond curls jumped rebelliously from her tightly braided pigtails immediately after her coiffure.

Today, in Aunt Albertina's honor, Fräulein tied a pink silk bow over her ears. Annemie was not happy because she had to sit still for an eternity. But the promising thought of the moor-kop in the kitchen bowl trumped all other considerations.

"Don't get dirty, Annemiechen. I have to fetch coffee for the ladies," exhorted Fräulein, after tying a house apron on the child. Annemarie felt her honor offended. She knew long ago that she must avoid filth; she had even taught cleanliness to Gerda.

"What game do we play until Fräulein comes back?" Annemarie asked, turning to her dolls and looking uncertainly around the nursery. "We can not make a racket because Aunt Albertina is so old and can't take it anymore."

Her gaze flew to a small book that peeped between the toy cabinets.

"Oh yes, decals."

Grandma had recently brought her the book. But Annemarie went for a walk in the fine weather, and had not yet come to withdraw the images. Now she did so fondly. First the white paper, then the excitement: What kind of image would turn up on the paper?

Annemie busily dragged her water filled soap dish to the children's table and pulled up a stool for Gerda so she could sit and watch how well her little Mama understood the work. A patch for moistening was not at hand. The girl used instead baby's diaper, hanging to dry on the flower board.

The sixty-four dollar question was where she should get a sheet of paper to draw off the pictures.

Brother Hans, who helped her amiably in such situations, was in school this afternoon. She didn't want to get involved with Klaus.

Why was her little table so white? It would work better than any piece of paper.

Slosh! She pasted the first picture on the table. Annemie slapped down on the image the entire water content of her soap dish, unconcerned with Doll Gerda's sodden curls. She re-filled the soap dish. Then she pressed with baby's diaper on the wet paper. But as the panties were tiny and didn't cover enough paper, Annemie, unconcerned, enlisted her clean house apron. She pressed it down with all her strength.

Cautiously, very cautiously, she lifted a corner of the wet paper.

"You see, Gerda, that's how it's done."

With hot cheeks Annemie pulled the paper off.

"Hurrah, the Struwwelpeter."[2]

Struwwelpeter was not complete. His long nails were missing, and his curly mane was cut by half.

But he shone unmistakably from the children's table.

---

[2] Der Struwwelpeter (1845) (or Shockheaded Peter) is a German children's book by Heinrich Hoffmann. Struwwelpeter is a slovenly boy who does not groom himself properly. The book consists of ten illustrated and rhymed stories, mostly about children. Each has a clear moral that demonstrates the disastrous consequences of misbehavior in an exaggerated way.

Annemie proudly showed the adoring Gerda her artwork before she went to the second image.

The evil Frederick with Sister Gretchen appeared above the Struwwelpeter.[3] It was a pity that the paper had moved, and that the dog and the beautiful liverwurst slipped onto Annemarie's apron instead of the white table top.

Zappelphilipp wriggled down from the table onto Annemie's pink batik sleeves.[4] The wet, blank paper stuck to the cheeks and forehead of the doctor's daughter and Gerda, like a magnificent wound plaster.

The little artist poured, in her zeal, all the water in the soap dish over Gerda and herself instead of the decal image.

Fräulein's voice rang out from the dining room: "Annemiechen, come and say 'Good day' to your aunt."

The child grabbed her dripping Gerda and hurried into the dining room.

---

[3] In "Die Geschichte vom bösen Friederich" (The Story of Evil Frederick), the second story of ten in *Der Struwwelpeter,* a violent boy terrorizes animals and people. Eventually he is bitten by a dog, who goes on to eat the boy's sausage while he is bedridden.

[4] In "Die Geschichte vom Zappel-Philipp" (The Story of Fidgety Philip), the eighth Struwwelpeter story, a boy who won't sit still at dinner accidentally knocks all of the food onto the floor, to his parents' great displeasure.

The moorkop and the marzipan potato—heavens! She had forgotten about them completely in her passion for the decals.

A quick glance at the cake basket revealed that the marzipan potato was gone, but the chocolate moorkop was enthroned there, a bit melted, in all its glory.

"Annemie, Lotte, look at you," Mom and Fräulein cried in horror with one voice, even before the child could make her curtsey to Aunt Albertina.

"I, oh God, I've probably splashed myself. I'm wet, but I'll be dry again" reassured Nesthäkchen. She greeted Auntie with a pat on the hand.

"Good day, my dear."

Aunt Albertina quickly drew back her delicate, small-veined hand, because the hand her niece offered was wet and sticky.

"Annemie, what did you do?" exclaimed Fräulein, who had gradually recovered from her fright.

"I made fine decal pictures, the Struwwelpeter and Zappelphilipp. You will rejoice, Fräulein," the girl said proudly.

"We enjoy the Zappelphilipp already," Mom said, holding Annemie's pink batik sleeve accusingly in the air. "Well, let's make you look human, and take the dirty paper from your face. You look like a wounded warrior. Aren't you ashamed to show yourself this way to your aunt? "

Annemie blushed to the roots of her blond curls. Yes, she was ashamed, not because of her visitor, but because Mommy rebuked her in front of her aunt. With a shy glance at Aunt Albertinchens old face, the girl saw that her aunt smiled and was amused. Nesthäkchen was comforted. Oh, Aunt Albertina was so good. She did not eat the moorkop. She had eaten the marzipan potato!

Fräulein led Nesthäkchen back into the nursery and gave her an earful en route. Annemie looked saddened that Fräulein was so angry with her. Yes, really, Mademoiselle was right, she was a careless girl. Annemarie had accused Gerda of the same carelessness, and then had not followed her own advice. But Fräulein would be happy when she saw the beautiful decals.

To Annemie's surprise, Fräulein was not overjoyed at the sight of the colorful pictures.

"For heaven's sake, you're a horrible child. Not only did you cover your pretty dress and your apron with ugly spots; you have totally spoiled your children's table. As punishment, you are not allowed back to visit your aunt," scolded Fräulein.

"Oh, dear Fräulein, I can not help it if no sheet of paper was available but the table was. Frida can wash it with soap. Auntie would be terribly sad if I did not come back. She might die. She is so old," cried Annemarie.

The final argument seemed to stir Fräulein. She tried to clean up Annemie for her visitor. But that was a difficult piece of work. The glued patches were painful to remove, but Annemie screamed quietly so Aunt Albertina did not fall into a swoon. Fräulein washed clean the girl's face and hands, put a flowery dress on her, and Annemie was ready.

But they did not go. Fräulein must be happy. The child could not abide her Fräulein's anger. The reconciliation was, from Annemie's side so stormy that her hair braid came undone. After her braids had been reconstructed, Annemie could compete with her Gerda.

"What do you mean, Gerdachen, whether the moorkop will be there?" she whispered in the ear of her doll excitedly.

The doll made a dubious face.

There it was, Annemie knew it: Aunt Albertina was a good person.

Auntie took without hesitation the small hand and kissed her favorite warmly.

"Now I like you, Annemiechen. So that's your new Gerda? Good day, my child."

Gerda made a well-bred curtsey.

"How old are you, little one?"

Gerda was silent, embarrassed.

"She's shy," said her mother.

After Aunt had entertained herself for a while with Annemie and Gerda, she turned back to Mommy. Nesthäkchen stood by and did what she had just forbidden her child to do: She let her blue eyes migrate between the marshmallow moorkop and Aunt Albertinchen's cavernous handbag.

Aunt seemed to have forgotten about her niece. Annemie found it appropriate to attract her attention.

"It took a long time, Aunt Albertina" she said with a mischievous smile.

"What, darling, my visit?"

"No but," she glanced at the handbag and did not finish the sentence.

"Lotte," said Mommy angry, "what are you begging for?"

Good Aunt Albertina laughed. "That's right, darling, you reminded me. When you are as old as I am, you forget so much." She pulled, to Annemie's enthusiasm, a delicious bag of chocolate cookies from her handbag.

The girl thanked Auntie with a blissful curtsey. It was much better that she had reminded Aunt Albertina than vice versa.

Annemie could go back to her children, but there was still something that captivated her: the marshmallow chocolate moorkop.

What were Mommy and Auntie waiting for?

Mom offered Aunt the cake bowl.

Annemie's heart trembled.

Aunt Albertina was a saint. She took a pretzel. But tomorrow she would certainly be confined to bed, the result of indigestion.

"Aren't you afraid that you will die, Aunt?" asked the little girl sympathetically.

"You think I'm so old, Luv?" Auntie asked puzzled.

"No, because of the many…"

Mommy's baleful stare prevented Annemie from finishing her hospitable speech.

"It's time for you to go back to the nursery," Mommy said emphatically.

Aunt intervened for her favorite.

"Leave her here a little while, I do so enjoy her," Aunt said, pulling Nesthäkchen to her.

So Annemie had to look closely at how Aunt tasted the pretzel. What a stupid custom that children received the leftover cake.

Mommy handed Aunt the cake basket again. Annemarie trembled. "Luv," Aunt insisted, "I can't eat another bite," but Mommy tormented: "A little bit."

Aunt Albertina accepted the cake without looking as she continued talking to mom.

Nesthäkchen's eyes were frightened, and Gerda was aghast.

It lay there; the beautiful moorkop, on Aunt Albertinchen's plate!

Boundless disappointment welled up in Annemie; tearfully she cried, "My moorkop! It's mine."

Gerda froze at the misbehavior of her small mom. Yet more shocked was Mommy. She didn't recognize her otherwise well mannered Nesthäkchen today.

Aunt Albertina turned in a friendly way.

"Oh, you want more?" With kind smile, she handed the child her plate with the desired moorkop.

Mommy intervened.

"Annemie deserves no cake today; she was too naughty. I had kept some marzipan potatoes, but they are only for good children."

Aunt Albertina implored, but Mommy remained firm.

The marzipan potato was for Hans, and the moorkop that Aunt Albertina didn't eat wandered into the stomach of Klaus.

Annemarie had to watch the great escape.

Chapter 11.
Nibble, nibble, little mouse

Rarely had a punishment made such a lasting impression on Annemarie, as the loss of the divine moorkop pastry. For days the sweet toothed girl was filled with deep regret that she was forbidden to eat the delectable brown chocolate. Henceforth, her favorite game was *confectioner*.

The flour and appetizer drawer in her doll kitchen was transformed into a pastry shop. Annemie tied a knot in each corner of her handkerchief, and voilà, she had the finest pastry chef's cap. Her Kurt got the cap. He became the pastry chef and was christened Zippel Hat Fritze.

The pastry shop was filled with tempting morsels. There were sand cakes in all sizes, baked every day in the park, fresh and thick, sprinkled with sugar. Begging Mommy for apples, Annemie made apple pie, apple strudel and apple torte in her small round metal baking form. From cardboard she cut tartlets and filled them with cherry pits. Chocolate cookies became impeccable chocolate cakes; marzipan potato was simulated with a regular potato served on a doily. But where should she find moorkop? Without moorkop a pastry shop was unthinkable.

Annemie had the strangest ideas. It was not long before she thought of taking her child Lolo and turning her upside down. The Moor doll had a Moor's head [Mohrenkopf or moor-kop]. But fortunately for poor Lolo, Nesthäkchen's eye fell on Fräulein's stocking basket.

The brown wool ball inside was indeed a magnificent Mohrenkopf. The dolls would lick every finger.

Now the game could begin. The Lord Pastry Chef put on her cap, arranged doll tables and doll chairs, in case someone wanted to drink chocolate or eat pastry, and let "Fritze with Zippel Hat" work as a waiter.

Ting-a-Ling rang the doorbell. The first customer came tripping in. It was Irenchen, but she played an old lady, and spoke in a trembling voice.

"What is your wish, madame?" The Lord Confectioner bowed politely to the ground.

"I want a cherry tartlet with whipped cream," ordered the old lady, her voice shaking. Annemie, pastry chef and guests rolled into one, had to play a person who was quite hoarse.

"Yes, madam, one moment, whipped cream is being prepared fresh."

The old lady took her place at the doll table. The pastry chef together with Fritze raced with Zippel cap to the wash room. There the Lord Confectioner with her little eggbeater from the doll kitchen produced in the soap dish a magnificent lather. This was blotted on the cardboard cherry tartlet and served by Fritze. Unfortunately, a corner of his slightly oversized stocking cap popped into the whipped cream. But that certainly did not disturb the old lady; she enjoyed her food anyway.

The Lord Pastry Chef had to serve a new customer.

This time it was a cute schoolgirl, Gerda, who was strapped into Irenchen's satchel. Immediately afterwards, another nice lady with a red umbrella set the shop bell in motion. The Lord Pastry Chef served only the lady. Children can wait.

"What does the lady wish?" The Lord Pastry Chef asked politely of the newcomer.

"For twenty pennies I would like crumb cake," demanded the lady, pointing with her hand to the apple pie on a piece of china.

"This is apple pie, my lady," answered the pastry chef obligingly.

"No matter, I am nearsighted," Mariannchen apologized with her glued eyes. She was the beautiful lady.

"Anything else, my lady?"

"Send me tomorrow a chocolate cake just around the corner, my name is Miss Magenweh [stomach ache], adieu,"

The lady disappeared.

"Tell me, my lady," Annemie imitated exactly the voice of the corpulent pastry chef who lived next door. She did not find the similarity entirely convincing, and stuffed a doll bed under her skirt to look stout.

"Lotte, I see you play beautifully. You are well-behaved today. I can love you," praised Mother in the next room.

Mother was with Fräulein. They were giving the summer wardrobe of her three offspring a thorough screening. The daughter had to entertain herself.

Nesthäkchen beamed from ear to ear at Mom's praise. Mother's recent dissatisfaction with her had lain heavily on her soul. Her shame during Aunt Albertina's visit rankled.

Annemie thought of her dignity and said with a deep bow: "Excuse me, ma'am, you're wrong, I'm Mr. Confectioner, not your Lotte! Does the lady wish a marshmallow?"

Mommy threatened with a meaningful smile, remembering the moorkop, and the Lord Confectioner turned her glowing face quickly to another customer. Why had she mentioned the silly marshmallow?

As Mom left the room, the deceptive voice of the stout pastry chef rang out.

"Honor me with another order." Mommy could not suppress her laughter.

The Lord Confectioner turned to the schoolgirl.

"Hey, little one, why are you crying?" he asked.

"Because no one has waited on me; I am here much longer than the myopic Miss Magenweh and Madame Mommy. If you treat all your customers so badly, we'll go to the new pastry shop in the other street."

"You're a naughty kid," said the Lord Confectioner disgusted. "Get out of here. Remember, for six pennies you can't get so many kitchen crumbs anyplace else."

Doll Gerda appreciated the rebuke. She bought pastry, despite the scolding.

After the brazen thing had left the pastry shop, no one came for a while. The Lord Confectioner was fatigued by her expenditure of effort. She sat down on a chair and consumed for refreshment an entire chocolate cake. Fritze looked enviously from under his Zippel cap.

Ting-a-Ling, the bell rang again.

A gentleman entered, a stranger. He was so black he must have come straight from inside a chimney. His name was Herr Lolo. Curiously, the chimney sweep wore short white embroidered knee pants.

He brought his daughter, a lovable baby. The child's mother was probably German. The little one was a bit dirty, but not nearly as black as the Moor Papa.

"What are you eating, my dear?" the Moor affectionately asked his daughter.

"Moorkop with whipped cream" responded the wise baby, even though it was only six months old.

"And the gentleman? Maybe a cup of chocolate?" suggested the chubby pastry chef who at once made three bows.

The gentleman thought for a moment.

"No, bring me a serving of vanilla ice cream." Sure, it was so hot inside the chimney that he wanted something cold.

The Lord Pastry Chef had little doll dishes in his ice house, which was Hanne's kitchen.

"Hanne, may I have a portion of ice cream, the gentleman from the chimney has ordered it," said the Lord Pastry Chef.

Hanne saw the need. She knocked off a piece of ice from the ice in the icebox and put it on the dolls' plate.

"Thank you, dear Hannah." The fat cook affectionately wrapped his arms around the fat cook and then hopped back into his shop. The ice bounced off the plate three times. But the pastry chef wiped it clean with his apron and served it to the Moor with a bow.

"One vanilla ice cream!"

Fritze with his Zippel cap, who should have had the whipped cream for the baby's moorkop, had been lazy and had done nothing. He got from his master a slap and was immediately dismissed from the service.

The Lord Confectioner brought the whipped cream, but made a mistake and put it on Mr. Lolo's Moorkop head instead of on the marshmallow moorkop on the plate.

Shouting and cursing Mr. Lolo's Moorkop ran out of the pastry shop without paying for the vanilla ice cream. He forgot his baby he was so angry.

Fritze took off his Zippel cap. He looked like a cute boy with a basket on his arm.

"A bread with caraway seeds, but not old," he demanded, and also at the same time put money on the table.

The Lord Confectioner looked helplessly at his shop. Heavens, the bread was all gone.

"A moment, my son, I'll get fresh bread from my bakery," and then he went into the kitchen.

"Hanne, Hanne love," but the kitchen was empty. The beloved Hanne seemed to have gone out with the trash.

You couldn't let a customer wait so long--impossible. The small confectioner ran himself to the bread box in the pantry, and because he was not allowed to touch a knife, he bored out with his finger a large piece of the sliced bread.

Then he put the bread carefully away.

Kurt wrapped his bread neatly in paper and put it in his basket.

A quadrupedal customer appeared in the open shop door. He immediately ran to the counter, where the succulent items were all so tempting. He put his hands, tucked into white fur gloves, on the apple pie.

"These goods must not be touched," said the pastry chef appalled.

But the Lord Quadruped did not let the rebuke bother him. Yes, he had the impudence to sniff a piece of cake.

"What do you wish, sir?" asked the confectioner for the third time.

The choice seemed difficult for the gentleman. Finally, he came to a decision. Instead of being served with cake at the table or receiving it packed in paper, he made short work of it.

Snap, Mr. Puck snapped up a huge piece of chocolate cake from the counter with his mouth and ran from the patisserie.

"Mummy, Mummy, my chocolate, my best chocolate cake," the Lord Confectioner rushed screaming behind the thief.

Mommy, who should summon the police, was not in her room. Hanne had brought her into the pantry, to show her that a mouse must be there. He'd eaten a sizable hole in the bread.

"Hanne, best you set a mousetrap," said Mrs. Braun.

"Nah, I will hunt the mouse myself. He's certainly here in the pantry. This afternoon the bread was whole." With that Hanne began searching zealously among the wooden barrels and jars filled with preserved fruits.

Nesthäkchen appeared wearing her pastry chef's cap. But in her amazement she forgot to point out the thief Puck to the police.

"Hey, what's going on here, are we pulling something out?" she asked curiously.

"No, we have a mouse in the pantry." Hanne dragged out wine and beer bottles. She left no object in place.

"A mouse, a mouse," cheered Nesthäkchen and jumped blessedly around between all the bottles and storage bags.

She forgot the thief, forgot the whole pastry business. "A mouse, a mouse," that was wonderful.

Annemie helped busily rummage through the pantry. She smashed the lid of the rice bin and let the onions roll out of the onion net. She noodled and spun under the kitchen cabinet and table, and secretly dipped her fingers in the sugar barrel. In this way she made herself extremely useful.

"If I get the mouse, he'll wish he'd never been born, forcing me to do such work," grumbled Hanne.

"What will you do to him, Hanne?" asked Annemie curious.

"I'll drown him alive!" Hanne said grimly.

Annemie felt sorry for the poor mouse. She wished Hanne would not catch him.

"Hanne, have you found your mouse?" Mommy stepped back into the kitchen.

"No, but I will. Imagine, in broad daylight to nibble a hole in the bread; such impertinence." She held the bread with the impressive hole in the air.

Annemie became pale, then purple-red.

Hesitating she looked from the bread to Hanne, and from Hanne to Mommy.

She swayed, she hesitated; she wrapped both arms around Hanne's wide hips and burst into bitter tears.

"You must not drown the poor mouse, Hanne, he can not help it. He has not eaten the bread. I took it. I was pastry chef, and wanted to buy my doll boy bread," lamented Nesthäkchen.

"You were the mouse? Just wait, if you think you're going to make such work for me again, mouse," the cook threatened amiably and straightened up her pantry again.

Annemie asked anxiously: "Will I be drowned alive?" Hanne, with a lively laugh, reached for a large bucket. Screaming Nesthäkchen took to her heels.

Chapter 12.
Sailor Girl Lina

Annemie's favorite walk in the Tiergarten was along the canal promenade. Ducklings swam to her when she threw in her breakfast bread. One duck was Annemie's favorite. He was much nicer than all the others. He had plumage that was red, green and yellow, and looked as if it was composed of nothing but doll rags. At first Annemie had thought the duck was not alive, just a toy. But as she continued throwing food to the other ducklings, he showed his vitality.

Hanne had to cut an extra bun for breakfast, so that the ducklings were fed.

Annemie admired many ships on the canal, small and large. They had stone blocks or coal loaded into their large wooden bodies.

As Nesthäkchen and Fräulein walked one day hand in hand along the waterfront, the girl saw her ducklings from afar. They formed large feather balls in the water, close to a vessel with bricks.

Annemie pulled out a roll. But no duck swam toward her, not even her special friend, colorful duck.

"Quack, quack, quack, quack, quack," said Annemie, smacking with her tongue. But the ducklings did not approach at this invitation.

"Duck, don't you know me? I'm Annemie," cried the grieved girl to the amusement of passersby.

"Throw them a piece of bread into the water. You'll see how quickly they come," advised Fräulein.

Annemie did as she was told. But no ducklings swam to her. The girl called in a loud voice: "Duck, there's liverwurst on it." Liverwurst did not lure the ducks.

Meanwhile Fräulein and Annemie came close to the cargo ships.

"Oh, now I know why your ducklings spurn their breakfast," laughed Fräulein, "Their table is set elsewhere. Look, Annemiechen, over there on the ship is a girl with a hunk of bread in her hand who feeds them."

"But they are my ducks." Annemie started to cry.

The girl on the ship heard Annemarie's loud wailing. She stopped throwing bread crumbs into the water, and marveled at the fine girl on the shore. Out of sheer amazement the boat girl forgot to eat her bread.

As the ducklings noticed that there was nothing more for them, they ungratefully swam shoreward to Annemie.

She hopped for joy.

"Well, there you are, all of you, do not be ashamed. Do I say hello? Should I have eaten my breakfast alone?" the girl chattered.

The ducks answered: "Quack quack quack," and competed with each other for the best crumbs.

"Look, Annemie, how cute the ship is that the girl stands on. Her apartment looks like a green house. What clean curtains hang at the window," said Fräulein, drawing Nesthäkchen's attention.

"Yes, and the pretty flowers that bloom in the large, green box, that is certainly her garden," said the girl. "Oh, please, dear Fräulein, let us go to the other side of the canal over the bridge. I can look at the ship close up."

Fräulein did Annemie the favor.

While they walked, the ducks escorted them. Fräulein was subjected to a barrage of questions.

"Why does the girl live on a ship and not in a real house, Fräulein?"

"Because her father is a sailor," was the answer.

"I wish my father were a sailor," said Nesthäkchen with a deep sigh.

"Why, child?"

"Then I should clatter around on the ship without you having the same fear that I would fall into the water. The ducklings would swim around me all day. Most beautiful would be that I could live in the cute cottage."

Nesthäkchen ticked off longingly all the benefits of ship life.

"Your nursery is much more livable," reassured Fräulein.

"Does the girl have a doll's kitchen?"

"I think not," said Fräulein.

"Does she have a mommy?"

"Yes, I am certain." Annemie was relieved at Fräulein's answer.

"A grandmother?"

This seemed to Fräulein dubious.

"I wonder if she has as many dolls as I?" asked the blabbermouth before Fräulein could answer the previous question.

"Annemie, you're a living question mark on two legs! Question the girl. We're close enough to the ship. "

The shy child would not. Nevertheless, Fräulein sat down on a bench near the boat to give Annemie opportunity for detailed observation of the vessel and its small inhabitant.

She was Annemie's age. She had two braided pigtails, but they were much blonder than Annemarie's golden hair. She wore a short red skirt and a blue apron.

"Like Hanne" thought Annemie admiringly. When she got closer to the sun-scorched, crumb smeared face, Annemie's admiration peaked.

Clogs, cute wooden clogs she wore, precisely like the ones Hanne tromped in when scrubbing and washing. Hanne's clogs delighted Nesthäkchen. When the sailor girl bent over, Annemie saw her red and blue socks. Annemie would never have thought that a child could be so lucky as to have clogs like Hanne's.

While the sailor girl filled Annemie's good heart with ardent envy, the sailor girl herself had similar feelings.

Ah, the fine white embroidered dress that the stranger wore, and the white hat with pink daisies: Lina, the sailor girl, thought they were charming. Lina liked Annemarie's white boots and white knee-length-socks too. She was mortally ashamed of her hideous clogs.

The two looked at each other in silent admiration.

But when their eyes met, Annemie had to laugh.

Lina nodded in a friendly way.

Annemie dared to start a conversation.

"What is your name?" she asked, putting her hands to her mouth and shouting, as though Lenchen was God knows how far away from her. In fact, the ship lay close to shore, and the girl had come up to the ship's railing.

"Lina," sounded back from the ship, "and you?"

"My name is Annemarie, but Fräulein calls me Annemie, and Father and Mom say Lotte to me when I'm good," cried Annemie, less stridently. She saw that she could communicate without much effort.

Of course, the fine girl on shore had three names. Lenchen accepted this fact readily. If you had such beautiful white booties, you could have three names.

"Why do you live on a boat?" Annemie continued her interrogation.

"Where else should I live?" Lina widened her blue eyes in astonishment.

"In a real home with stairs," Annemarie instructed the country child.

"Our ship has a flight of stairs!" The flaxen blond stood proudly on the small staircase that led down to the living room.

Oh right, that was cute, like a doll apartment. Annemie understood everything. "Do you have a porter?" she asked.

"A porter?" Lina stammered. She had never heard the word *porter*. "Are you thinking of a satchel?"

"Oh, no," laughed Annemie, "Don't you know what a concierge is? Do you know what an emperor is? "

"Yes," Lina nodded. Her protruding pigtails flew up to heaven. The Emperor she knew.

"Well, a porter is something like that, guarding the house, so no thief comes in," instructed Annemie.

"Oh, now I know." The sailor Lina jumped for joy in the air, and the small wooden clogs clapped together wonderfully.

"We have Karo, a doorman who guards the ship against thieves." As if she had called him, a yellow pooch appeared beside Lina.

Annemie shook with laughter.

"A dog is no porter!" she exclaimed, laughing uncontrollably. "We have a dog. His name is Puck. I have six dolls. Do you have dolls?"

Of course, Lina had a doll. She immediately ran down, with clattering clogs, to bring it up to Annemie. Before she had dug up her doll, Fräulein took Nesthäkchen by the hand in order to move on. From afar Annemie could see the small red dressed child waving a greeting.

"I have a new girlfriend, Lina, and she lives on a real ship!" There was no one in the whole house to whom Annemie did not communicate this important news. Even Puck and Antics had been informed

Klaus was interested. He had many friends at school, but unfortunately not one lived on a ship.

"Father, if you were a sailor, I would love you more," said Nesthäkchen after she said goodnight.

"Lotte, what does that mean?"

"I would not need to sleep in the ol' nursery and might, like Lina, sleep in the cute room on the water."

"We can change places, Lenchen's father and I. He makes my patients healthy, and I steer his ship. Would you like that, Lotte?" laughed Dr. Braun.

The next day Doll Gerda came to the Tiergarten, to be presented to Sailor Lina.

When Annemie opened her eyes in the morning, she tormented her Fräulein: "Let's go to see Lenchen."

As they turned into the waterfront, Lenchen's red skirt glowed at them. She seemed to have been waiting for her new friend.

"Fräulein, dearest, best Fräulein, sit down, please, on the bench," asked Annemie, "I will entertain myself with Lenchen."

"The bench's too sunny. I'll get sunstroke," said Fräulein undecided.

"Oh, it doesn't hurt when you get sunstroke, Fräulein." The girl looked at her seriously. "The other day I had so many mosquito bites that sunstroke wouldn't itch." She pointed to her bare arms.

Fräulein laughed.

"If you promise me, Annemie, to be a good girl and not to climb around on the fence, I will sit down here on the shady side of the path."

"How shall I climb over the fence, Fräulein? The guard comes and brings me to the police," Annemie whispered with shy respect.

Fräulein knew she could rest easy. Nesthäkchen was scared of the Tiergarten guard.

Annemie could continue her friendship with the sailor girl Lina.

This time, Lina's mother appeared. She had equally beautiful wooden clogs as Lina, and hung laundry on the ship; it looked funny. Then she went back into the small kitchen, which was next to the living room. Smoke whirled happily from the thin chimney to heaven, indicating that she was cooking lunch for Lenchen.

Meanwhile, the girls had shown each other their dolls. Lina stared with admiration at the fashionable Gerda, who wore a rose red dress. Gerda looked proudly and condescendingly at the poor doll of the sailor's child.

Such an ol' thing: it had no hair, but a black painted on porcelain wig. It didn't have a decent dress, instead, an ol' ragged calico skirt. Gerda was much finer.

Mama Annemie was nicer and less proud than Gerda. She asked gently: "What's your doll's name, Lina?"

When she heard that Lenchen's doll was called Gustel, a native of the Oderberg fair, she said: "You see he's worldlier than you, Gerda."

Ashamed Doll Gerda abandoned her stupid pride and looked curiously at the well-traveled Gustel with black porcelain hair.

Annemie and Lina fed the ducks together, the colorful duck out-eating the others.

Annemie had cherries with her for breakfast. Lina made covetous eyes as she noticed the two beautiful, dark red twin cherries that hung like earrings over each of Annemarie's ears.

"Would you like one?" asked Annemie kindheartedly.

Lina nodded.

Annemie threw a cherry from the shore to the ship.

Whiz--something flew from the grass embankment. A cheeky sparrow won.

But the second cherry that Annemie hurled with all her strength reached its goal. Lenchen began cheering in her blue apron.

What a fun game. Annemie threw cherries at Lenchen until the bag was empty. In between throws, Annemie, every few minutes, emerged on the footpath to show Fräulein that she was still there.

Annemie and Sailor Girl Lenchen saw each other almost every day, always friendlier. The dolls became friends, too.

One day Lenchen sadly said, as Annemie reappeared on the shore, while Fräulein took her place on the bench, "Today we go back."

"Back where?" asked Annemie.

Lenchen laughed at her friend. "To Oderberg, to grand-mother."

"When do you leave?" Annemie looked startled.

"Soon, Father is getting ready."

On the ship Annemarie noticed lively activity.

Annemie felt sad saying goodbye, for the first time in her young life. "Are you coming back soon, Lenchen?"

"I do not know." Lina saw how her friend grieved.

"I do so much want to give you something, at least a kiss, but we can not each reach other." Annemie threw affectionately a kiss to Lenchen.

"I have absolutely nothing that I could give you. You've got everything, much more than I," said Lina, who in her pretty muslin dress was astounded at her friend's obvious affluence.

"You have something that is much, much nicer than anything I've got," said Annemie, glancing at Lenchens feet, "your sweet clogs."

"These ol' things? I will gladly give them to you, Annemarie; in Oderberg Grandmother has another pair." A small wooden shoe flew toward Annemarie's feet.

She could not believe her eyes.

"Should I keep it, really?" she asked, blissfully stroking the shoe.

"Sure," and its brother made the journey through the air to shore.

"I will give you my white boots." Looking around, Annemarie took off her expensive canvas boots and—whiz--they flew like two white doves over to Lenchen.

She made an equally blissful face as Annemie's. The two children, delighted with their new shoes, did not notice that the ship slowly began to move.

When she was separated several meters from shore, Lina shouted: "We're under way, adieu, adieu, Annemarie."

"Adieu, Lenchen, farewell, come back soon!" cried Annemie behind the departing ship, and she waved her clogs. Lina waved back with the costly white boots.

Suddenly it occurred to Annemie that she could accompany her friend Lina a bit further. She ran wearing the clogs and fell flat on her face. Yes, Annemie, everything has to be learned in life, even running in clogs.

As Annemie crawled back to her feet and dusted off her dress, Lina was long gone. Annemarie would need some clog training. She must learn to walk like Hanne and Lina in the clogs; otherwise she would be too slow to accompany Fräulein.

Annemarie paced back and forth. Amazed strollers watched the dear child in the white muslin dress, pink silk sash, and strange footwear. Some stopped, shaking their heads, and observed the tentative steps.

Annemie tumbled at least half a dozen times onto her nose, in an effort to learn her new art. She went quickly to Fräulein.

Tramp, tramp, tramp.

Fräulein looked up in astonishment.

"Oops, Annemie, you can't run until you give Lenchen her shoes back. Your fun is excessive," scolded Fräulein

"But Fräulein, the sweet wooden clogs, please, please, let me keep them, I can use them when you clean house," pleaded the girl.

"Where did your white booties go? Did you leave them on the shore, you careless girl?"

"Please, Fräulein," protested Annemie, "I have traded them to Lenchen for her clogs. She was pleased."

"Immediately you must bring Lenchen the wooden clogs and get your good boots back. You're not at all clever, you silly child." Fräulein ran to the shore.

Clomp, clomp, Annemie followed behind.

"But Fräulein, Fräulein, Lina is no longer there. She is in Oderberg with her grandmother," cried the little one, who had to stop. She had lost a clog running.

"What? And she took your beautiful booties with her?" Fräulein made a horrified face.

"Yes, of course, but I do have these fine clogs. They're a thousand times better." Lovingly Annemie gestured toward her footwear.

Fräulein raced along and did not answer. Maybe she could catch the ship. But it was, if not yet in Oderberg, no longer to be seen.

Clomp, clomp, clomp, Annemie trekked behind.

"What shall I do with you? I can not walk home with you." Fräulein cast a puzzled look at Nesthäkchen's strange looking feet.

"I can run in them," reassured Annemie. The girl could not imagine that anyone should be less enthusiastic about her wooden clogs than she herself.

Fräulein was mortified. No, she would not walk with Annemarie. They hailed a cab home.

Nesthäkchen was overjoyed. First, the sweet wooden clogs, and a cab ride to boot.

The pain of parting from Sailor Girl Lina disappeared.

Chapter 13.
Nesthäkchen Takes a Trip

"What? My Lotte wants to leave me alone tomorrow and fly out into the wide world?" asked father, taking his Nesthäkchen tenderly on his lap.

"Mommy remains here with you," consoled Annemie, "and you both go to Switzerland. But if you ardently wish, Fräulein and Klaus can go to see Aunt and Uncle on their farm. I would rather go with you."

"Is that what you want?"

"Yes, terribly." Annemie wrapped both arms around her father's neck.

Doctor Braun was touched.

"Is it hard for you to separate from us, Lotte?"

"Oh, heaven forbid," Annemie's laughing face showed no pain of departure, "but you know, Daddy, in Switzerland, I can eat Swiss cheese all day long, as much as I want. I love Swiss cheese. I love to eat the holes."

With that Nesthäkchen jumped up, because she had so terribly much to do before tomorrow.

Fräulein and Mommy packed the suitcase in the nursery. Annemie fetched her doll basket and crammed in the clothes for her children. When the basket was full she looked around.

"Fräulein, do you still have a lot of space? I can't get in Irenchen's school satchel or baby's bottle," wailed the doll mother anxiously.

"Annemiechen, what do you want with all that stuff? Aunt Kate has you two crabs. You're enough," laughed Mommy.

"Yes, but my children want to visit the country. Irenchen desires red cheeks, Mariannchen should be able look into the green with her sick eyes, and Lolo needs fresh air. Baby will grow big and strong in the rain, and Kurt, the rascal, can run riot. I cannot part with Gerdachen! "

"What? You want to drag along half a dozen dolls to Aunt Kate's house?" asked Mom, who tried in vain to keep a straight face.

"Yes, of course, she will be happy, and Cousin Elli, too. She is twelve years old."

"No, Lotte, you can not. One doll you may take, the others remain here. You choose," said Mommy with an edge in her voice.

Nesthäkchen looked dismayed. The dolls sat with disappointed faces. They had been looking forward to the trip.

Leaving her children is a difficult task for a mother, but she had no choice. It was necessary that the pale Irenchen should make the journey to the country, Lolo too. Frida might not care for them properly.

Annemarie's eyes fell on Gerda. The doll sat on her stool and looked at her mom anxiously.

"Gerdachen, do not be afraid, you're coming with me. How could I separate myself from my sweet Nesthäkchen?" cried the girl, pulling her favorite doll to her heart.

Annemie felt tugs at her own heart, when she thought of separating from Mums, who whispered, "And I have to give up my youngest," with tears in her eyes.

"I'm giving you so much Swiss cheese!"

Should Mom think of Annemie's comfort, or of Father, whose job was so hard? He needed to recover without his lively offspring. Mom wiped her tears and quickly continued her work. The children, left with her sister and Fräulein, would get excellent supervision. Hans, the oldest, was to make a walking tour with his gym teacher and several other boys.

"Fräulein, you did a wonderful job, but you forgot something, right?" Panting Nesthäkchen dragged up her huge doll carriage, when the suitcase was almost full.

"Annemie, we can not take that big thing, or Antics either." Half amused, half angry, Fräulein grabbed the birdcage with Antics that Annemie dropped in the trunk, in the middle of her beautifully ironed summer dress.

"My Gerda must go for a walk and Antics will starve if I do not give him food and water," asserted the girl as she threw her clogs into the suitcase.

Fräulein had difficulty to convince her that Frida was well equipped to care for Antics, and that Gerda would prefer her cousins' small wagon. Perhaps in Arnsdorf Cousin Elli's old doll carriage was in the attic. The wooden clogs they could spare, as Annemarie would surely not scrub floors.

Klaus, the second young traveler, appeared, under one arm his butterfly collection and under the other his fortress with all its regiments. He asked Fräulein to pack these items in the suitcase because they were too colorful to leave behind.

Butterflies, fortress and all regiments wandered back into the boy's room, along with Klaus. Annemie was sent on a visit to Hanne, because the girl would have to do without her for so long. Fräulein finally had a quiet room in which to pack. The dolls could sit and watch.

The day before the trip was so gorgeous that travel seemed superfluous. Father and Mother were more tender than usual. Hanne let Nesthäkchen go through all her storage boxes, because she would no longer be there tomorrow. Hans gave her an eraser. His sister was so impressed by his generosity that she lovingly jumped on his back and exclaimed: "I wanted you to come to Arnsdorf, Hänschen, and Klaus to travel with his teacher."

In the next room sat one doll that the other dolls stared at jealously. Doll Gerda wished a thousand times more ardently than Annemarie that Klaus was going off with his teacher. She did not look forward to summer recreation with the wild Klaus nearby.

That evening Grandma appeared to say farewell to her grandchildren. She brought them a large bag of biscuits for the trip and they were thrilled. Annemarie was uncontrollable. She was intensely excited. She romped with Klaus among hat boxes, suitcases and chairs, until Fräulein threatened not to take her. When she lay in her bed she prayed fervently: "Dear God, I ask that tomorrow comes quickly."

God obliged. When Fräulein awakened Annemie an hour earlier than usual, the girl was tired, as though she had just fallen asleep.

"Annemie, the train leaves." cried Fräulein.

Oh, Nesthäkchen was out of bed as though lightning had flashed before her sleepy eyes. Gerda jumped out with both feet at the same time.

Today getting dressed went twice as fast. If you want to travel, the water is not as wet as otherwise, the comb does not twinge as much, and two cups of cocoa are swallowed without appetite.

"Fräulein, the train goes," Annemie reminded Fräulein, and the former could not move fast enough. Long before the coach arrived, the girl was ready to leave, wearing on her right arm travel-ready Gerda, on her left her teddy bear, on which she put Kurt's hat and Irenchen's blue cape.

"Is this young gentleman going along?" asked Father, amused at beholding the strange traveler.

Annemie assented eagerly because she could take a doll, and animals would be welcome on a farm, where there are many oxen and cows.

"Yes, but bears do not belong on a farm," argued Mom because Nesthäkchen wanted to take the teddy bear as a traveling companion.

Father's objection, "He gets no red cheeks in the country air," did not help, only Fräulein's energetic remonstrance: "Then you stay at home."

The bear wandered back to the abandoned dolls. After Hanne and Frida promised Nesthäkchen to care for the poor, motherless children, the girl was finally able to make the trip with her Gerda.

Klaus, the green specimen box hanging off his shoulder and the butterfly net waving like a flag in his hand, was enthroned on the box next to the driver. The parents went along to the station.

Oh, how glorious is traveling: Hanne and Frida waving from the balcony, the Lord Concierge himself helping load the suitcases, and the car horns tooting so wonderfully.

With shining eyes Nesthäkchen rode to the station, where another pleasure awaited. Grandma had arrived to say goodbye to her sweetheart Annemie. Grandmother handed a small travel bag with candies for Doll Gerda; the doll served as a proxy. They were surely intended for her little Mama.

Father and mother did not want to let go of the arm of their Nesthäkchen.

"Be obedient and well behaved, Lotte, Klaus. Fräulein writes me a letter every day about your behavior, think about it if you consider doing something naughty. Greet Uncle Henry and Aunt Kate warmly."

The stationmaster gave the signal.

"Toot! All aboard!" cried Annemie while Mommy looked with tearful eyes at her children. Filled with happiness, Nesthäkchen rode into the wide world.

The trip was not long for the children. Gerda unlocked her mouth and nose. There was so much to see outside: first, a large, dark forest where Little Red Riding Hood had met the wolf; then, a village with a red church and many cute houses, like those Annemie had for her dolls; now came a meadow with beautiful red, blue, white and yellow flowers. Oh, if Annemarie could only pick them! The train rattled on, unconcerned about Annemarie's desires, ratteratta ratteratta puff puff puff ratteratta, on and on.

"Oh, many, many sheeps over there." The girl clapped her hands in delight.

"This is a flock of sheep," Fräulein instructed, "and the old man with the long stick is the shepherd."

"Annemie, you're a sheep, they are not sheeps but sheep!" Klaus thought it necessary to teach his sister something.

Apart from this kindness he behaved quite well, because he was busy almost all the time stuffing food into his face.

Gerda, for the first time of her life, was quite happy. Klaus, opposite her, blinked his brown eyes mischievously, but she gradually lost her distrust. She did not recognize the boy today.

But the doll had rejoiced too soon.

The three sat peacefully. The farms and trees became boring. With a sincere face Klaus asked his sister: "You, Annemie, let's play *Wind*."

"Oh yes, Kläuschen." Annemie had had enough of the fields and meadows that looked all the same.

"Whee!" said Klaus whistling, "whee!" Doll Gerda's straw hat flew out the window into the middle of a field of red poppies.

"My hat, my beautiful hat" cried Gerda, or was it Annemie? "The train has to stop. You must not go on, you ol' train!" Bitterly the girl cried.

The train rattled on, untroubled by Annemie's and Gerda's yammering: ratteratta ratteratta puff puff puff ratteratta, on and on.

And it sounded as if it was laughing at Annemie in the bargain. Or was it the naughty Klaus who laughed up his sleeve?

When Fräulein scolded him, he opened his big mouth: "Why does the stupid thing yell; she wanted us to play *Wind*."

Fräulein said with a straight face: "Remember my letter to Mommy, Klaus." Klaus became quite sheepish and was transformed into a true paragon of virtue.

Gerda got a stocking cap made from Nesthäkchen's handkerchief. She could not possibly arrive without a hat in Arnsdorf. What would the cows have said?

Annemie busied herself looking at a lady sitting in the corner who had her eyes closed.

"My aunt is sleeping," she told Fräulein loudly.

"Shhh!" said Fräulein and put an admonishing finger to her mouth.

The lady moved restlessly, but did not open her eyes.

"Auntie still sleeps," Annemarie said after a while, a bit more subdued, but still loud enough for Fräulein to lay anew her finger to her mouth.

The sleeping lady opened her lips, and gentle snores emerged: "Chch CHCHCH chchchch pfff pfff," that sounded almost as sonorous as the railway music.

"Aunt is snoring," whispered Nesthäkchen with bright enthusiasm.

A special grunting: CHCHCH chchchch pff pfff began. The train produced a "ratteratta puff puff" at the same time. Klaus and Annemie were startled; then they both laughed out loud.

The startled lady opened her eyes.

"See, now you have disturbed the lady," said Fräulein with annoyance. "Pardon, ma'am."

"No matter," the lady smiled gently and closed her eyes.

"You know what, Annemiechen, you must sleep a bit," suggested Fräulein, rubbing her own eyes, and taking Nesthäkchen on her lap.

"No, I can not sleep; otherwise the old wind comes back and ends up blowing my Gerda out of the window." The girl threw a meaningful look at the innocent Klaus with Grandma's candy basket.

"I'll take good care," Fräulein soothed the travel-fatigued child. Annemie closed her eyelids, and after a while Fräulein did the same. Doll Gerda was not asleep, sitting upright in her corner, keeping watch.

She watched as the useless Klaus carefully broke the gold cord of Grandma's candy basket. One sweet after another walked into his mouth.

"You're snarfing my sweets!" Tearfully the doll pulled her sleeping mummy's pigtails.

As the aunt had previously, Annemie awoke. She sprang up frightened and crying, and awakened Fräulein.

Klaus got a slap on the hands and Annemie a piece of chocolate from the lady, who had rested.

They arrived. Fräulein sat Annemie's cap on her head, and Annemie adjusted Gerda's handkerchief cap.

The train stopped. Uncle Henry stood on the platform and greeted Annemie and Gerda with laughter. "Well, child, are you there?" he said, lifting his niece from the compartment. Then he gave Klaus a tender pat: "Still the same Bandit as before, boy?" and took the travel bag from Fräulein.

They went to his carriage. You had to drive over an hour to get to Arnsdorf Farm. On the box sat at attention, in his blue coat with bright buttons, August, the coachman. He put his hand to his cap.

Nesthäkchen curtsied in deep reverence before him. He looked so much more distinguished than her porter in Berlin. Klaus patted the two bays on the back, although Annemie did not quite trust them. Klaus lifted himself to the box next to August, and begged him for his whip. He snapped it happily as the wagon bounced along the dirt road.

"You see, little one, that's a windmill, where the miller grinds his grain, and from there, the Grasberg, you can spin down merrily.

These are our meadows. They will soon be hay." Uncle Henry entertained his niece, whom he held lovingly on his lap.

The blabbermouth fell silent amidst all the tantalizing sights. Fräulein nodded at him smiling. Uncle looked at Annemie more closely.

Holla! The girl slept. Her blond head had curled up tightly in Uncle's sleeve, her cheeks were flushed and her mouth was open. The long journey had fatigued her. Doll Gerda had closed her eyes. Fast asleep, the two small travelers made their entry into Arnsdorf.

Chapter 14.
Cock-a-doodle-do, the cock is already awake.

Over the dewy meadows of Arnsdorf the morning wind blew. He looked into the farm, where everyone was sound asleep. The golden red rooster, sleeping on the dunghill, opened half an eye and blinked sleepily in the morning breeze. The rooster puffed his arrogant face, tore both eyes open and flapped his golden red wings, ringing out to the skies "Cock-a-doodle-do, Cock-a-doodle-do." The cock narrowed his eyes, because he knew his song by heart.

"We woke up the deep sleepers," thought the morning wind and rattled against the window of the guest room, which was above the courtyard.

The guest room stirred. A childish leg stretched to the sky and then disappeared under the blanket. The morning wind looked surprised. Oops, who was in there in the crib: a strange girl and a strange doll that he had never seen here on the farm. The face of the little one was still buried deep in the cushions.

The morning breeze understood awakening people: that was his job on the farm. He took a willow branch hanging on the wall and struck it happily against the windowpane.

The visiting girl put her second leg out, and arms too, but went back to sleep.

The morning breeze signaled his friend, the rooster, who did not hesitate long. Once more sounded, "Cock-a-doodle-do."

The girl dreamed that the cock in her box of toys was alive and had crowed loudly. But when the cock on the dung heap sang for the third time "Cock-a-doodle-do," she sat up straight in bed.

Oh, the sweet little thing, how amazed she looked around her new environment! The sight of her pleased the morning wind exceptionally.

Annemarie remembered where she was.

In Arnsdorf, correct. But how did she come here to bed? She could no longer recall. She was so tired yesterday she could hardly greet Aunt Kate, Cousin Elli and the other cousins.

"Cock-a-doodle-do," the rooster called. "Cock-a-doodle-do" rang out in bright tones that caused Doll Gerda and Fräulein to lurch upward.

"Annemie, child, what are you thinking? Lay down and sleep," exclaimed Fräulein.

"Cock-a-doodle-do."

"'The cock is awake. We must get up. A good sleep is not as long,' says Frida." Annemie, who arrived yesterday and got to bed early, was completely rested.

Unfortunately Fräulein was tired.

"Be quiet, little heart, and do not disturb me," she said.

Annemie promised because she loved her Fräulein.

She began an audible conversation with Gerda.

"Do you like it, Gerdachen?"

The doll shrugged. She could not judge fairly in the short time she had been here.

Meanwhile, the morning wind had awakened the doves in the dove cote.

"Rrruck rrruck rrruck rrruck girrr" they cooed and raised their heads.

And "rrruck rrruck rrruck rrruck, the doves are up" they cooed from their cote.

"Annemie, you promised me to be quiet," moaned Fräulein.

That's right. She had totally forgotten.

"Are you afraid of the moo cows, Gerda? They do not bite!" Annemie continued her whispered conversation with the doll.

The cows had awakened. The doll crawled timidly under the pillow.

But her little Mama laughed and made a much more beautiful "moo moo uh," which did not overjoy her weary Fräulein.

For a while it was quiet. Fräulein believed the girlish troublemaker had fallen asleep. Fräulein slept deeply on her other side.

"Baa baa baa" sounded outside. This time Annemie thought that she should not awaken Fräulein, as much as she would have liked to bleat along. She held her mouth closed. But as the bleating did not stop, Annemie no longer could stay in bed.

One two three she was at the window, Gerda with her.

"Oh there are so many sheep."

How funny they jumped, hop hop, for they were out to pasture. The servants were up. They harnessed the wagons to go into the fields. In the middle of the yard Uncle Henry stood, looking after things.

What? They were all already up, the cock, the deaf moo cows, the sheep, the servants and even Uncle Henry.

Annemie would remain upstairs no longer.

A quick glance at Fräulein's bed told the girl not to worry. Fräulein was fast asleep. Like the wind, the little one was out the door, her doll child in her arms. She jumped joyously down the stairs.

"Good morning, Uncle Henry. Please, give me one of the sweet sheep, you've got so many," she called out behind the lord of the manor.

He turned amazed.

Two dear ragamuffins stood before him. Gerda had not dressed either.

"Crab, Fräulein will be furious. You'll catch cold." Uncle pulled off his loden jacket and wrapped Annemie and Gerda inside it. Then he took them both by the arm.

The servants all around were laughing. The bleating sheep sounded as if they were laughing too.

Uncle carried the two back into the house.

"I don't want to go back to the guest room," begged Annemie, "please, please, dear uncle! Fräulein is so terribly tired, and I disturb her," added the little fox.

"Yes, where shall I leave you, crab? I have to ride into the fields."

"You can take me with you, Uncle Henry. I have often ridden on Klaus' large rocking horse. I ride on father's shoulders many times. I do not fall down."

But Uncle seemed not quite comfortable with the proposal.

"Let's see if Aunt Kate is free."

Yes, Aunt Kate was free. She laughed uproariously, as Uncle put the lively package in her arms.

"Well rested, Luv?"

Annemie did not answer. She studied Aunt Kate's face.

"Oh, Aunt Kate, you look like Mom. You must not scold me even though I ran away from Fräulein."

That did not deter Aunt Kate. She laughed even more.

"What will I do with you, Luv? You can't walk around in your night clothes, and we do not want to bother Fräulein.

Wait, I got it. There's a full washable suit for Peter that will fit you."

"Oh yes, fine" exulted Annemie. Aunt Kate took her to her bedroom. She washed and combed the well behaved girl. She wanted to slip as quickly as possible into Cousin Peter's pants.

Fräulein, with anxious face, appeared downstairs. She had searched for her ward everywhere in vain. A cute boy with two blond pigtails stood in front of her and laughed mischievously.

Fräulein could not be angry. Annemie looked too sweet. And she asked tenderly, "Fräulein, you want to take a short walk?" Fräulein could not refuse her.

Twelve year old Elli appeared. She gave Annemie a pat on the pants and said, "Well, Peter." Not Brother Peter but laughing Annemarie embraced her.

The boys shared a room. They didn't recognize Annemarie. They said a loud hello.

"Where do we go first?" asked the ten year old Herbert at breakfast.

"Of course, the stables, we must show Klaus and Annemie the horses, cows and pigs," cried his younger brother Peter.

"No, I want to see the attic," said Annemarie seriously.

"What? What are you going to do in the attic?" they asked.

"I must dig up Elli's old doll carriage for my Gerda," said the doll mother.

But the good Elli had asked that her doll carriage be set to rights for her cousin; and her full sized cooking machine too.

From that moment, Annemie loved her cousin Elli beyond measure.

After Gerda had been trans-formed from a ragamuffin into a de-cently dressed doll, the whole group headed to the stables.

Fräulein could now unpack at leisure.

First they saw the horses. A servant set the bold Klaus on one of the bays, and Klaus shouted, "Gee" and "Hott."

Annemie stood watching anxiously from afar. She did not dare to approach the cute filly, *Baby Horse*, that Elli fed sugar. When she was persuaded to hand the animal a lump of sugar, she drew her hand back screaming; the colt had sniffed it. She counted carefully to see if she lacked any fingers, and the sugar lay on the ground.

With the cows Annemie fared not much better. Nevertheless, her Gerda assured her boldly: "They do not bite," but Annemarie dared not approach. Why did they beat so annoyingly with their tail puffs? They had four legs for pushing, one on every corner.

The girl cried out delighted at a pretty white brown cow and pointed: "This is the cow from my picture book."

"Nonsense," laughed Cousin Peter, "this one is alive."

"It's her sister, she looks exactly as much like her as Aunt Kate looks like my mom," said Annemie with certainty.

Uncle Henry, who had returned from his morning ride, and had heard the flattering comparison, roared with laughter.

"Do you know what the cow gives us?" he asked.

"My Gerda knows that. You get milk from the cow," Annemie exclaimed proudly.

"The coffee, where does it come from?" teased Uncle.

The girl thought a moment.

"From the horse, of course, because he is brown!"

Peals of laughter followed. Even the cows were laughing, their long tails wagging back and forth.

Annemie ran out of the barn and told Elli that she was "terribly shy."

The pigs did not attract the little cousin. She said contemptuously: "They're not really pigs! The piglets in my storybook look rosy and do not smell awful! "

Annemarie loved the poultry nursery.

Oh God, how cute: the ducklings with yellow downy feathers, the tiny goslings, and the chicks that tapped their way behind the mother hen.

The rabbit hutch with its exuberant residents, who tumbled happily, pleased the city child.

"Let's go into the garden," said Elli.

Ah, there it was beautiful. Colorful pansies, forget-me-nots, and many daisies grew on the grass.

"Pluck whatever you want to make a wreath for your Gerda, Annemiechen" suggested Elli.

The girl hesitated.

"May I walk on the lawn?" she asked.

"Of course," laughed Elli.

"Are there guards here, like the guards in the Tiergarten?" The Berliner looked around cautiously.

"Annemie, here you can walk wherever you want," said her cousin.

"Oh, that's nice of you. I will never return to the ol' Tiergarten," Annemarie said jubilantly, like a bird that flies for the first time from its small cage into the open air.

Klaus had grasped his rural freedom quickly. He was first in the hammock and first on the swing. He struggled on the high bar, and then went to the cousins' currant and gooseberry bushes.

Next day he had a sick stomach.

Chapter 15
"A bird flew in"

Gorgeous weeks the Berlin children spent on the estate. The days passed much faster than at home. With both hands

Klaus and Annemie held each other. Every day brought something new and nice.

Klaus looked like a real bandit, sunburned and tattered. No tree was too high and no digging was too deep. Fräulein's summer recreation consisted of daily patching of panties.

Annemie had become an able tomboy. She hung around everywhere with the three boys. Her fear of horses, cows and pigs was long gone. The turkey sat down before her respectably when he got sick. Nesthäkchen was sick too but recovered. Her cheeks were as red as her muslin dress and her legs as brown as her brown stockings.

The gentle Gerda was completely out of control. She sat in her pretty dresses on fences and bushes, got blows to the head that left bumps, appeared with a scratched face from the thorns, and usually came home barefoot.

If she had not recovered as well as her little Mama, it was not the Arnsdorf air; Klaus was to blame. The rascal gave the doll no peace; forever she had to tremble before him.

When the children went with the handcart out into the field, Klaus jostled and shoved. He rolled Doll Gerda through a ladder rung and left her lying on the road. Not even her mother noticed, until the return trip, when she retrieved the dusty doll.

When the children played in the hay, Gerda was close to suffocation. The evil Klaus buried her alive under a giant hay mountain. He bombed poor Gerda with green apples which the wind had blown to the ground. Her nose was flattened. When the children set their boat afloat in the duck pond, Gerda ended up in the greenish water. And if Herbert, hearing Annemie's yell, had not saved her, Klaus would have drowned her miserably or forced her to eat a frog. Oh what fear Gerda had of the croaking green fiends!

Once again Doll Gerda suddenly disappeared. One moment she had played "robber and princess" with Annemie and other children in the grove; then she was up and away. Annemarie, full of anxiety, searched every bramble, every molehill. Gerda did not appear.

"It is terrible for the child. In Arnsdorf she is totally wild," she complained to Elli, Gerda's aunt. "Who knows where Gerda is now?"

The boys, Herbert and Peter, who were the robbers, waved their handkerchiefs as peace flags. They came up to ask if the girls had seen their robber captain Klaus. Annemie knew where she had to look for Gerda.

"My child has been stolen; the robber captain has stolen my Gerda." Lamenting, Annemarie went with the others to search.

Nowhere was a trace, either of Klaus or Gerda. The searchers rummaged through the rose hedges, the arcades, yard and house.

The doll thief was gone. In fact, he sat on the top floor of the granary and peered through a skylight scornfully at his pursuers.

But where had he left Doll Gerda? She was no longer in his company.

When the robber captain left the poor doll child, Gerda thought her last hour had struck.

"Dear God," she prayed, "let me die at least a gentle death. Make sure that the bad Klaus does not drown me in the duck pond with the green frog fiends! "

Klaus raced with the abducted child over hill and dale. The doll fainted; she closed her eyes. She did not see what the bad guy was doing with her.

When she dared to finally open her eyelids, she pinched her nose with her celluloid hand to see if she was alive. Where was she, in heaven?

No, she couldn't see the sky. A faint twilight illuminated the room through which blew strange warm air. She heard an odd hum. Her doll heart beat with fear well into her neck.

Doll Gerda could actually be quite satisfied with her situation. She rested in a comfortable wooden cradle on soft, green grass. But she wanted to know where she was.

As the humming increased beside her, Gerda held her breath.

Merciful Heaven, a terrible monster appeared next to her, with bulging eyes and cloven hoof, a cow!

Good God, she would be devoured in the next moment, skin and hair! Poor Gerda knew at once where the evil Klaus had dragged her: the manger of the cowshed.

Why were the monsters waiting? Why was the cow not eating her? At least the misery would come to an end!

But the cow did not intend to eat Gerda. The cow had as much fear of the doll as the doll had of her. With anxiously bulging eyes she stared at the strange food in her crib.

Suddenly Doll Gerda felt taken up. She did not dare to open her eyes. The monster had her between its teeth.

"Farewell, Annemiechen, I thank you. You've been so sweet to me and cared so well for me," thought the doll.

She heard a human voice: "My goodness, not even the servants know what they are doing here. Look at what they poured into the fodder," and then a booming laugh. "Oh, it is Annemarie's doll, which the cows could have eaten for supper!"

It was the squire who inspected the cattle feed.

Gerda squinted through her lashes. No, she was not, as she feared, between the teeth of the cow; Uncle Henry had her in his fingers. He put her in the inside pocket of his jacket. Oh, how sheltered the half-dead, frightened doll felt near Uncle's chest.

Behind them joy roared forth. The cows could eat their supper.

The family sat together on the rose covered veranda at dinner. The bandit chief Klaus showed up.

Annemie forgot her strawberry milk and grabbed him by the lapel of his jacket.

"Klaus, where have you left my Gerda?"

The boy made a mischievous face.

"The princess sits trapped in a cave," he said.

"You old robber, think about what you've done, my sweet Gerda is frightened to be alone," lamented the doll mother.

"What ransom are you paying?" The robber captain led the negotiations.

"My new top and a ladybug and my whole glass of strawberry milk." Annemie cried because Klaus shook his head.

Doll Gerda overheard everything in Uncle Henry's pocket. Uncle was properly moved by the self-sacrificing love of the small mom.

Uncle got down to business.

"Forget it, Bandit, you produce the doll immediately without any ransom, or you'll get no strawberry milk."

Klaus obeyed. He had profound respect for Uncle Henry, and he loved strawberry milk. With a shocked face he appeared a few minutes later.

"It's terrible what happened!" He blurted.

"What, what?" cried everyone.

"The cow has eaten up the doll! I had it hidden in the manger, and now it is empty."

"My poor Gerda!" Annemie's tears flowed in streams, and Klaus began to howl. He did not get the strawberry milk, and blame plagued him. His sister was suffering terribly. He didn't have a bad heart; he was a rollicking kid.

Annemie and Klaus mourned the devoured Gerda. Meanwhile, a clear fine laugh came from Uncle's coat pocket. But no one listened.

As Annemarie sobbed painfully, she felt soft curls on her wet cheek. Affectionately a small, cold face snuggled against her.

"Gerda, you're alive." The brightly joyous Annemie held her unharmed child in her arms.

Uncle Henry had the weeping bandit chief by the collar.

"This time I have the saved the doll, but woe to you, you rascal, if you damage a hair on Gerda's head."

Klaus promised solemnly to leave Doll Gerda henceforth in peace and received his strawberry milk.

The shock had cured Klaus. He left the doll totally alone. But he persisted in his wild pranks in spite of everything. Even his little sister he deceived.

It was the day before returning home. Aunt Kate had her coffee circle visiting, a company of twelve different ladies every week. Several women from neighboring farms and others from the nearby town belonged to it.

Since the weather was so beautiful, Aunt Kate had covered the coffee table in the open air under the large walnut tree. Elli had diligently helped and Annemarie eagerly wrapped the teaspoons and napkins.

"Children, you can play in the grove this afternoon. We will not hear you romping," said Aunt Kate to the three boys. "But Annemie can stay with me; Elli goes into town for piano lessons, and Fräulein wants to pack."

"Too bad we can not be at the tea party," Herbert said with a regretful look at the rose decorated table.

"Yes, Mademoiselle baked cakes and beat whipped cream," Peter remembered sadly.

"No, I don't mean that," the elder Herbert said. "But they laugh so volubly at a tea party. You can hear them God knows how far away. If I could be there! "

"You can, yes," Klaus commented with serenity.

"No, Mother said we should play in the grove."

"You must not be seen," said Klaus, the smallest but most cunning of the three.

"We might be able to hide under the table," thought Herbert.

"No, since you came, the tablecloth is not large enough." Peter shook his head.

"Up here in the walnut tree nobody will see us," whispered Klaus.

The walnut tree it was: yes, fabulous.

"But what do we do with Annemie?" Herbert thoughtfully furrowed his brow.

"We'll take her along. She has learned to climb trees." Klaus knew what to do.

Annemie immediately accepted the proposal. Shortly before four o'clock, one child after another climbed on the bench and from there into the low branches of the large, dense walnut tree. Even Annemie accomplished the feat with Herbert's help.

"My Gerda must make the journey up the tree." Annemie clapped her hands in delight. "It's fine's up here, like a green arbor!" she said.

"Psst," said Herbert to her. The first ladies arrived.

Annemie held Gerda's mouth as a precaution.

The birds in the green branches had a long wait until the party was complete, and the housekeeper appeared with a large coffee pot.

She put the giant bowl of whipped cream into the middle of the table just under the walnut tree. Peter, the gourmet, licked his lips. Herbert, Klaus and Annemie, the other birds, craned their necks and perked up covetous beaks.

Actually, it was terribly boring at a coffee klatsch. The ladies did nothing more than eat, drink and talk. Now and then they laughed too, but not so much as Herbert had said.

Oh how much nicer it would be to play in the woods and fields, rather than to sit up here so perfectly still, and be bored half to death.

Every single one of the five birds, Doll Gerda included, wished that Klaus would never have come up with the scheme, Klaus most of all. He thought, in all seriousness, whether he could not secretly slip down behind the tree.

"Your children leave tomorrow. Will it be difficult to separate from them?" the fat woman mayor said to Aunt Kate.

"Oh, yes," she answered, "I will miss little Annemarie, Klaus, the scoundrel, less. I'm happy every day when he comes home in one piece."

You see, Klaus, there you have it. The fly on the wall has to hear about his own disgrace.

Annemie could not sit still. The branch on which she was sitting began to crack. Doll Gerda had trouble keeping quiet. They dangled their legs.

"Oho, what is that?" On a lady pharmacist's nose something jumped down from the tree and fell to the ground, something small and brown.

"It must have been a nut," Aunt Kate reassured the frightened lady.

Gerda craned her neck above her gold beetle shoes.

Wham, she lost her balance and fell upside down from the tree, right into the whipped cream.

The coffee klatsch ladies screamed in fright.

Only the fat woman mayor retained her sense of humor.

"What kind of bird is that?" She laughed and fished Gerda from the whipped cream.

"That's Annemie's doll. Her mother will probably not be far off," said Aunt Kate and peered into the walnut tree.

Right she was. A pair of childish legs hung down. A pitiful little voice called: "Please, Aunt Kate, get me down."

Amidst general laughter the second bird appeared.

"Annemie, what were you doing up there?" asked Aunt Kate, as her niece was happily back on her feet.

"We wanted terribly to be at your coffee klatsch, but it was mighty boring!"

The ladies laughed at the uncomplimentary criticism. Aunt Kate asked in astonishment: "We? Who do you mean?"

"Well, the three boys, Gerda and me." Once more Aunt Kate peered into the walnut tree, but no bird could be seen.

The three had long flown off in the general turmoil. The nest was empty.

That was Klaus' and Annemie's last adventure in Arnsdorf. The next day they went home.

Chapter 16.
In kindergarten

Nesthäkchen was supposed to start school in October. She had registered. But the urban girls' school nearby was crowded, and her parents did not want to send the girl to a private school. Annemie was reserved for Easter; Mommy was glad to keep her youngest home during winter.

But there were days when Mommy wished Annemie had begun school in October. The parents were pleased to see their children sunburnt and rosy-cheeked, but not so pleased the kids had become wild after the unrestrained country life. For Klaus, yes, school was the best medicine, because he had to re-learn to sit still, but Nesthäkchen was hard to tame at home. She could not get used to city life.

The hall door had to remain closed, so that Annemie did not go out without her hat and coat, which she had done in Arnsdorf. On the balcony she could no longer be left alone; she had climbed just as high in the trees in Arnsdorf as on the building fence. During office hours father had to keep his door firmly closed; or his daughter would suddenly appear and state, with no regard for the patient, that she would help him cure people.

In the Tiergarten the guard was no longer a dread personage. Annemie jumped over the fence and ran onto the grass behind her ball, though Fräulein warned her not to. Fräulein now had her hands full with the tomboy.

The dolls were surprised and displeased at the transformation of their little mama. Rarely did Annemie bother with them; she would rather romp and stomp. Kurt had to go for a week with a hole in his sock. Irenchen got her hair combed less than weekly. Mariannchen's eyes remained glued shut. Lolo was dirtier than before, and baby did not thrive; she lacked maternal love. Annemie did not pick up the dolls. She did not let them go for a walk in their garden, or even to bed, the poor creatures. Mostly they were scattered around on the hard floor.

The poor Irenchen spent the night under the wardrobe, starving. The bad doll mother had no time to cook for her children. Irenchen had to climb on the table, jump to her feet and kick up a row. Only Gerda, the favorite doll, was not neglected. In all the girl's stupidities, Gerda was her faithful companion.

Worse was when the beautiful summer weather came to an end, and ugly, gray rainy days arrived. Annemarie was unable to walk to the park and had to stay at home.

The little girl had not experienced boredom; the hours dragged on, and she had forgotten how to sit still.

"Fräulein, what shall I do?"

"Mom, I'm terribly bored." So it went all day.

"You'll have to take care of your dolls' clothing, Anne-miechen," suggested Fräulein. "Look how dirty your children are."

"Ah, the ol 'dolls," grumbled Annemie, listlessly struggling against ennui.

"Play with your pretty shop. You've much to keep you busy," Mom said, shaking her head.

Annemie ran to Hanne and begged her for all sorts of things for her store; when the game should have started, it was over.

"Fräulein, I am so bored," sounded anew.

Reproachfully the dolls observed the little nuisance. They would have liked to help Annemie pass the time, but she wanted nothing more to do with them.

"I wish you were at school, Lotte," Mom said with a deep sigh.

Nesthäkchen was of the same opinion; then at least she would not get so bored as she did at home.

One day, Annemarie was once more unendurable. She had no interest in her toys. Mom was fed up.

"You're going to kindergarten, my child. At least you'll be busy mornings," she said.

Kindergarten? What was that? The word "garden" produced in Nesthäkchen memories of the beautiful Arnsdorf farm garden. In Arnsdorf, she could romp to her heart's content on the lawn and could climb trees and pick fruit, as much as she wanted. The fact that more children were in this garden tempted Annemie. She was a changed girl. The whiny mewling had stopped. She shouted jubilantly: "Tomorrow I'll be in kindergarten."

Mommy brought her Nesthäkchen to school herself. It was a private kindergarten in the neighborhood, recommended to her, with ten children.

Where is the garden?" asked Annemie, vainly looking around when they ascended two flights of stairs in a home.

Mommy could not respond because the door had opened when she rang.

A charming young lady came to meet them.

"I want to sign up my little one for your kindergarten, Miss Gebhardt," Mom said. "She has not started school due to over-crowding and can no longer stay home."

Annemie blushed. Now the strange lady knew how naughty she had been at home.

But the young lady leaned down amiably to the kid, stroked her cheek and said, "We will certainly be good friends. I'm Aunt Martha, and we will play together nicely." Then she opened the door to the next room. "See, here is our kindergarten. Here are more little girls and boys. Will you wish them 'Good day'?"

Not Annemie; shyly she stood in the doorway, her index finger in her mouth, and threw a fearful glance into the next room.

Should there be a garden? In the room two little girls played with dolls, several small boys had coupled together chairs to make a railway, and shouted, "all aboard!", while two other boys built a large tower from blocks. At the table sat children who eagerly bent their heads over colorful weaving.

"Best you leave me your little one, madam, and she will acclimatize fastest," said the young lady.

Mommy was quite agreeable.

She leaned down toward Annemie, kissed her and said in a minatory tone, "Be good, my Lotte, this afternoon Fräulein will pick you up."

Mrs. Braun was not out of the room when a deafening howl sounded behind her.

"Mommy Mommy, don't leave me." Annemie wrapped her arms around mom and hung on tight.

"Lotte, do not be so stupid, the other children are without their moms and do not cry," Mrs. Braun calmed her Nesthäkchen.

"Come, I'll show you something very beautiful," comforted Aunt Martha, and pushed a piece of chocolate in the crying girl's open mouth. The candy was more consoling than views of the Magnificent.

The young lady fetched a glass ball in which stood a cute doll house. Annemie watched curiously as Miss Gebhardt inverted the ball.

Oh, fine, it was snowing. Large, thick white flakes flew into the glass ball around the cottage.

Annemie clapped her hands with joy, her misery forgotten.

Meanwhile Miss Gebhardt had given Mommy a sign to leave the room. When Annemarie turned around to show Mom the lovely snowy house, Mom wasn't there.

Screaming, Nesthäkchen wanted to run after her. But Aunt Martha had wrapped her arm around the girl.

"Don't you want to come to us in the kindergarten?" she asked.

"There's no garden, merely an ol' room!" cried Annemie malevolently.

Aunt Martha looked at her sadly, and the children all made frightened faces. Oh, Annemarie was ashamed.

"Now let's all play together in a circle," said Aunt Martha, as if she did not see the embarrassment of the girl. "Can you suggest something, Lotte?"

"My name is not Lotte," she said, still tearful.

"What else? Your mom called you Lotte," marveled Aunt Martha.

"Yes, Father and Mom call me Lotte, but only when I'm good, otherwise I'm Annemie," she said.

"Then be good so that I soon can call you Lotte. And now we'll play "Sister, come along." Take hold of the little boy, Annemie."

Five minutes later, no one would have thought that Annemie would have ever cried. Her face was filled with delight.
Happily she jumped with the other children around in a circle.
She no longer noticed that it was a room, and not a garden,
where she played.

Aunt Martha was so nice. She knew pretty games, "Rotten
Egg" and "Dumb Wave" and the comical game of "Mi ma
mouse man."

"Are these all your children, Aunt Martha?" asked Annemie amidst the playing.

"No, that would be a bit much," laughed Aunt Martha,
"They are lent to me."

"Oh, I have six children at home," said the girl eagerly, "but
Gerda is my favorite, my Nesthäkchen. She is wonderful."

Annemie stood on her toes, stretched her arms and
showed Aunt Martha Gerda's size.

"Bring us your Gerda tomorrow. We'll get to know her
well," Aunt Martha said, smiling.

"What? Gerda is allowed to come to kindergarten?" Bright
happiness shone from Annemie's blue eyes.

"Of course," nodded Aunt Martha, "you see, Erna has
brought her Bubi and Milly her Toni with black braids. Today

you can be their nanny. Tomorrow you will be a mom and show us your child. "

That was a fun game. Nesthäkchen, who at home no long-er loved playing with dolls, was proud to be "Fräulein" for Milly's Toni and Erna's Bubi in the kindergarten. Every few minutes she said to Toni, "You're a terrible nuisance; play games like the other children and don't say, 'I'm bored.'"

When Fräulein appeared to pick up Annemie, the girl cov-ered her face.

"What, already? We play so beautifully!"

"Tomorrow you'll play more. Now you must eat lunch." Aunt Martha stroked tenderly Annemie's blond head.

Annemie, one two three, wrapped her arms around the neck of the young lady and whispered, "I love you, Aunt Mar-tha!"

"I love you too, my dear, because you are so pretty, adieu, Lotte," said Aunt Martha.

Blissfully Annemarie hopped through the street, holding Fräulein's hand. "Aunt Martha loves me, and she calls me Lotte, because I'm so terrible mannerly, and tomorrow I may bring my Gerda." One thought was more beautiful than the other.

"Well, Annemie, how was it in kindergarten?" asked Brother Hans at home.

"Wonderful, beautiful!" cried the girl enthusiastically.

"Did they have refreshments?" asked Klaus interested.

"Yes, chocolate," exulted his sister.

Mommy was happy that her Nesthäkchen was so well-liked. She had had a heavy heart, leaving her wailing child in kindergarten.

Even Fräulein was pleased because Annemie was not bored in the afternoon.

The girl didn't torment her once. She had far too much to do. She had to spiff up Gerda for her kindergarten debut. She washed her panties in the small washtub and ironed them with her cute doll iron. What would Erna's Bubi and Milly's Toni say if Gerda appeared with dirty panties in kindergarten? Irenchen's small school apron went to Gerda. Then the child brushed the doll's tangled curls. She couldn't imagine Gerda as Struwwelpeter.

"Are you looking forward to tomorrow, Gerdachen?" asked Annemie at night as she kissed her child.

The doll made a radiant face, but Nesthäkchen beamed more.

"You do not have to be stupid and howl when Fräulein leaves," said Annemie the next morning to the expectant doll on the way to kindergarten.

No, Gerda was not nearly as stupid as her little mom yesterday. She cried a bit. Annemie held her out to Aunt Martha with the words: "I want my little one to be happy in kindergarten because she can no longer keep busy at home." Gerda curtseyed and gave each child a "good day" with her celluloid hand.

Today, when Gerda was there, it was even more beautiful than yesterday. Annemie built a house for Gerda, and the crab pushed Gerda toward it with her foot. She learned to fold a bookmark of red and golden glossy paper, a gift for grandma. And the second bookmark of light blue and silver paper was for Aunt Albertina.

The first bookmark did not materialize. The paper had the naughty property of jumping from the folding needle and tearing.

Impatiently Nesthäkchen threw it out. She saw that all the girls, even the boys who were much younger than she was, had no problems making the bookmark. Thereupon, ashamed, she attacked the problem again.

She permitted Aunt Martha to call her "Lotte."

Gradually the colorful striped bookmarks did not jump from the needle, and the paper was no longer annoyed when Nesthäkchen pulled it. Oh, how proud she was, when the first bookmark was ready for Grandma! And Gerda was almost as proud of her clever little mama.

Then was the reward for the hard work. Aunt Martha sat at the piano and sang funny children's songs: "Span along Hansel," "Noodle thick maid," "Donkey and the Devil". All too soon Fräulein came to pick up Annemie and Gerda.

On the third day, with Nesthäkchen and Doll Gerda, Puck appeared in kindergarten.

But instead of politely wagging his tail, he snapped angrily at Aunt Martha. Little Maxie jumped and began to shout. The dog snapped a piece of ham from small Herta's breakfast bread. Such an unmannerly fellow Aunt Martha did not need in her kindergarten. Fräulein had to take him home.

Nesthäkchen learned from Aunt Martha how to occupy herself. She never complained about boredom at home. One thing Annemie had learned: to worry like a real doll mother about her children. The dolls had no need to complain about their mother. Annemie would be half dead with shame before Erna and Milly if she had brought in bedraggled dolls.

The most wonderful times of the week, to Nesthäkchen and Doll Gerda, were the three mornings in kindergarten, even if it was not a real garden!

Chapter 17.
Tap tap, Knecht Ruprecht comes

It was the hour in the evening when Knecht Ruprecht came listening at the doors of nurseries.[5] Did a child deserve a Christmas gift or only a rod?

Many a tomboy was tame, because Knecht Ruprecht noted everything in his book, each bad habit, and Christmas gifts were apportioned accordingly.

Nesthäkchen was particularly likeable in the weeks before Christmas. Even with Klaus she got on reasonably well so that all her Christmas wishes would be fulfilled.

Fräulein sat with a large piece of paper and a long pencil at the nursery table. She wrote out all Annemarie's wishes that the girl dictated to her, so Knecht Ruprecht wouldn't forget a thing.

"A small clinic like Father's," Nesthäkchen began her wish list.

---

[5] Knecht Ruprecht (English: Farmhand Rupert or Servant Rupert) is a companion of Saint Nicholas, described in the folklore of Germany. The companions of Saint Nicholas are a group of closely related figures who accompany St. Nicholas in German-speaking Europe and more widely throughout the territories formerly in the Holy Roman Empire. These characters act as a foil to the benevolent Christmas gift-bringer, threatening to thrash or abduct disobedient children.

"Annemiechen, Knecht Ruprecht cannot bring you something like that; it doesn't exist for children," laughed Fräulein.

"Yes, a little doll clinic, and I'm the Doctor, please, please, write it down, Fräulein. Knecht Ruprecht, who is so wise, will know what I mean," begged the girl, full of tenderness.

Fräulein emblazoned on top of the list: A small clinic.

"Then I would like so terribly to have a mini-Wertheim Department Store, but with a proper elevator and a refreshment room for my dolls. And a toy warehouse, too," Annemie wished further.

"Child, if you have no other desires, Knecht Ruprecht will laugh his head off at us," Fräulein objected, shaking her head.

"Well, the others are the same," comforted Annemarie. "I need a cute little doll carrier and a small fountain. I want Knecht Ruprecht to bring me, please, a doll kindergarten, like Aunt Martha's."

Nesthäkchen frowned and thought hard.

"And for your children do you want anything? You're quite a selfish little mother," helped Fräulein.

"Oh, for my doll children I need a ton. For Irenchen I order red cheeks, a corset for Mariannchen, along with a new pair of eyes, brown they should be, and a small umbrella. Lolo might use two new thumbs because hers are cut off, and a white feather hat. Don't you think, Fräulein, it will make her dark face stand out? And my Kurt needs two new legs, a right arm and eyes that close. He is not a rabbit that must sleep with his eyes open. A specimen box, like the ones Hans and Klaus have, would make the boy happy. Babychen needs to get short dresses and pearly whites. This Christmas she is three years old and doesn't have a single tooth. Now for my youngest. Come, Gerdachen, what do you wish for? Tell me; whisper in my ear."

Annemie grabbed her Gerda. She had recently bathed the doll and put a bathrobe in the doll carriage, so that she should not catch cold.

Horrified she let her favorite slide back into the pillows.

"Fräulein, Fräulein," Annemie was pale with fright, "come over here. Gerdachen is bald."

Unstoppably the tears flowed down Annemarie's cheeks.

Fräulein pulled the white wagon curtain back. Gerda was totally changed. Her horrified mom stared with uncomprehending eyes. Quite small and miserable Gerda's face had become, because her curly wig was missing. It lay beside her on the pillow. Gerda had a big hole in her head.

"It's not so bad, Annemiechen, the wig was washed off by the bath water," Fräulein soothed the excited child.

"Oh, my poor, poor Gerda, how hurt you must feel. I can see her whole brain and all the thoughts in her head," wailed Nesthäkchen.

"Father makes her a bandage," comforted Fräulein lovingly," and Knecht Ruprecht brings her new hair. Would she be pleased with braids?"

"No, buns, she is grown and comes with me to kindergarten" sobbed Annemie distressed.

"All right, then I write down: hair bun for doll Gerda. What do you mean? A red sports jacket: Grandmother has already knitted you one, Annemie." Fräulein tried to distract the child from her grief.

"No, a dear green one," mused the troubled doll mama, who continued to cry. "But if Knecht Ruprecht forgets the hair bun, my poor Gerda will go through the world bald for her whole life," wailed Annemie anew.

"He will not forget, Luv, I've written it down, and, if necessary, I can remind him," reassured Fräulein.

"Do you speak with him, Fräulein?" As Annemie listened, her tears began to flow more slowly.

"Of course," nodded Fräulein. "Four weeks before Christmas, he asks me every night whether you've been naughty or nice that day."

"Will you tell him everything, Fräulein, every time I cried?" asked Nesthäkchen sheepishly.

"Of course, I have to tell him the truth," said Fräulein.

"The fact that today I cried over Gerda's bald head: you'll tell him that?"

"Yes, but he will not be angry. You were not naughty. You cried because you were filled with compassion for your child," was the reassuring answer.

"Be careful. Don't let him, even accidentally, stick you in his bag, Fräulein!" Nesthäkchen made a half-frightened, half-mischievous face at the thought.

"I'll be careful," laughed Fräulein. "In the evening, don't you want to put your shoes in front of the door for Knecht Ruprecht, like Elli, Herbert and Peter in Arnsdorf. He will fill them at Christmas, Annemie."

"Yes, I know, Fräulein, I want to terribly. If children have been good during the day, Knecht Ruprecht always puts a golden thread and spice cookies in the shoes, and if they were naughty, a silver thread and nothing else. Klaus says Knecht Ruprecht does that only in Silesia. Our Berlin Knecht Ruprecht does not, because it is not the custom with us. "

"Darling, there is only one Knecht Ruprecht for the whole world. He's one and the same in Silesia and Berlin," instructed Fräulein.

"Even for America?" Nesthäkchen shook her head in disbelief.

"Of course, even for Africa."

"I want to know how he can visit, in an evening, all the children in Berlin, America, Silesia and Africa," said Annemie excited. "He must have Seven League Boots or at least an airship."

"Probably an airship," decided Fräulein about the difficult question. "I have heard it sometimes hum in the evening. I would at any rate try your luck, Annemiechen. Put your shoes in front of the door. Then you see whether Knecht Ruprecht knows the custom or not."

That was obvious. Nesthäkchen absorbed a lot more than usual today. Klaus found the transformed Gerda. Jubilantly he danced with the little bald head in the room and sang. "Gerda has lost her braids, now she looks clipped." Outraged, Annemarie gave him one punch, not the two she wanted to inflict. The decision was momentous.

Father skillfully made the doll child a bandage. Gerda looked like the Arabs from the Arabian Nights. Mommy put a sizable piece of chocolate on Gerda as a patch, which healed the pain of her small mom at the same time.

In the evening Annemie carefully placed her red house shoes for Knecht Ruprecht outside the nursery door; and next to them her doll shoes. All her children were going to have a gold thread and spice cookies. The shoe assortment included Gerda's gold bug shoes, Irenchen's patent leather shoes, Mariannchen's brown laced boots, Lolo's white leather shoes, baby's knitted wool booties and the wild Kurt's  hole-filled boots. The other shoes hovered God knows where.

Annemarie waited with bated breath in bed next to Gerda.

Both listened.

Where was Knecht Ruprecht? Annemie wanted him to eavesdrop so terribly!

Surrrr rrrrrr

The two clearly heard a loud humming outside in the courtyard.

"You, Gerda, do you hear, that is Knecht Ruprecht's airship!" whispered Annemie excited.

But Gerda shook her bandaged head: Nonsense, that was merely the elevator!

No, certainly, it had been the airship, for now there was a tap tap with heavy boots down the corridor to the nursery door.

"Do you hear him?" asked Annemie, hardly daring to breathe.

But Gerda disagreed with her little Mama: That could just as well be Frida who took all doll shoes for cleaning.

In vain Annemie perked up her ears. Nothing more could be heard, neither Knecht Ruprecht nor Fräulein's voice talking to him.

Oh God, if Fräulein forgot to tell Knecht Ruprecht that Gerda needed new hair. The poor thing would spend her life disfigured. This idea almost broke Annemie's soft heart.

"No, my child Gerda," she whispered tenderly, while her tears welled up in her eyes, "you shall not go around bald! With bald head, with no hair, you cannot appear in kindergarten. The other dolls will laugh at you. I'll give you one of my braids. I've got two."

And before Doll Gerda could stop her, Annemie was out of her crib and groping for the nursery table.

There Fräulein had left her sewing basket with the giant scissors.

Ritsch ratchet snip snap went the scissors, like cutting a rat tail. Blissfully the girl jumped back to bed.

"So, Gerdachen, no longer do you need to be sad, now you have nice braids like mine." Nesthäkchen fastened her clipped pigtail with a hair ribbon to doll Gerda's bandage.

Gerda snuggled gratefully with her good little mama. Each of them slept peacefully with her one pigtail.

The next morning the happiness turned into tears. When Fräulein came to Annemie's bed to dress her, she was as shocked as the girl had been yesterday at the sight of her doll.

"Annemie, for heaven's sake, what have you done?"

Fräulein stared at Nesthäkchen. The girl looked half like a girl, half like a boy. For a moment she did not think about the cut pigtail.

"What did you do with your pigtail?" Fräulein could not believe her eyes.

"My Gerda grew it overnight." With beaming face Annemie held the doll up. But there was no sign of a ponytail; only the bandage sat on her head.

Yes, where had the pigtail gone? Annemie began to search, while Fräulein stood completely frozen.

"There it is!" From under the pillow the girl pulled her clipped braid, which Gerda had lost in her sleep, and hopped happily around in bed.

Fräulein came back to life.

"You should be ashamed, you bad child, you cut your hair, oh, what will Mom say?" Fräulein raced out of the room to inform Mrs. Braun of the remarkable transformation of their Nesthäkchen.

"I wanted to make my Gerda the gift of a ponytail. She can not run around with an ugly bald head." Tearfully Annemarie twisted her smiling face, as Mommy, agitated, entered the nursery.

"Lotte Lotte, how you look." Mommy was as shocked as Fräulein. "Do you not know that you may not touch scissors, you naughty girl? Now I must cut the other braid off, it cannot stay! "

Annemie's faint cry became a loud yammer.

"No no, I must keep my ponytail. I will not go with an ugly bald head to kindergarten." She screamed so loudly that Father came to see what was wrong with his Lotte.

As Father heard the terrible story of the truncated pigtail, he laughed aloud.

Quite surprised, Nesthäkchen turned her tearful eyes on him. Was Father not angry like the others?

No, Father took his little one's arm, wiped her tears and said soothingly to Mommy, "Our Lotte did not mean any harm; she wanted to help her child. Mother's Love thinks never of itself, and the hair will grow back."

But Father could not save his favorite from the hairdresser with the large scissors. Her head could not stay the way it was.

Ritsch ratchet snip snap went the scissors as the other pigtail was amputated. Bitterly Annemarie cried in the barber shop.

Fräulein grasped the ponytail carefully, and Annemie glanced into the large mirror.

"I look like Klaus, abominable," she sobbed, "Knecht Ruprecht will think that I'm a boy and bring me a mess of ol' soldiers for Christmas."

"A rod he will bring you and nothing more because any-thing else you surely do not deserve," said Fräulein determined.

"What did he put into my shoes?" Only now Annemie thought about the shoes. In her excitement she had forgotten all about them.

Alas! In Annemie's red shoes there was no gold thread and no spice cookies, not even a silver thread. But all the dolls had golden filaments and spice cookies in their shoes, even the wild Kurt. Knecht Ruprecht seemed to know nothing about Anne-mie.

"No, Lotte, I can not love you." Mommy held her eyes closed when her youngest reappeared with a close-cropped head.

"I would have been glad if my Gerda had a bald head!" said the girl half tearful, half reproachful.

She won Mrs. Braun's maternal love. Mother took her Lotte on her lap and gave her a kiss of forgiveness.

The little girl promised solemnly never to do it again.

Yes, Annemie, that will be difficult, because braids do not grow back as soon as they are cut off.

Fräulein brought out hat and cloak. It was time for kinder-garten.

Annemie, who otherwise gladly visited Aunt Martha, didn't want to go at all.

"I'm shy. Aunt Martha will think I'm a boy!" she whispered in Fräulein's ear.

Fräulein said, "It's nothing that you are ashamed; this is your punishment!"

"Father at least could put a bandage around my head, as he did for Gerda," Annemarie pleaded.

But father had gone to his practice. Two little bald heads, Annemie and Gerda, appeared before Aunt Martha and the kindergarten children, the surprise of the day.

Oh, Annemie was ashamed. Everyone asked her where she had left her pretty braids.

Nevertheless, the children finished their cute Christmas work at Aunt Martha's. With clear voices they sang Christmas carols. Annemie did not enjoy herself. The song "Tomorrow comes Santa Claus" she dared not sing because Knecht Ruprecht did not want to know of her.

A few days later a small bald head was gone. Doll Gerda vanished. Despite Annemie's anxious search Gerda did not reappear.

Whether Klaus had taken Gerda, or Knecht Ruprecht had, was to Nesthäkchen a mystery.

Chapter 18.
Dolls' Christmas

Faster than Nesthäkchen thought, it was Christmas Eve, the most important day of the year. Knecht Ruprecht did not know where his head was. Was this an incitement to arrive just in time with all the dolls, soldiers, toys and story books on earth? His sled broke through the snowy winter forest. Knecht Ruprecht is an old-fashioned man. If there is snow, he comes on Christmas Eve not in an airship, but as he has from time immemorial; in his giant cloud sled he slides down to the ground.

In the back of the carriage, the seat was full of toys loaded into sacks. Two angels with silver white swan pelts and frozen red noses kept watch. No doll came to harm and no soldier fled.

As for the two angels, one heard quite clearly how voices whispered about what was in the bags. Of course, they were the dolls. Ladies always have something to chatter about.

"I'll certainly be in a castle for a little princess," said a doll, which was almost as big as a child and wore a pink silk dress proudly. "She cooks me my favorite dishes every day: chocolate soup and raisin roast with marzipan potatoes."

"I do not go to a castle," said another doll that had a simple cotton dress. "A little princess has so many dolls; a new one wouldn't mean much to her. No, I want to go to a poor girl who loves only me."

So each of the dolls spoke of her hopes about where Knecht Ruprecht would take her. Some wanted the country because it was healthy, others found it more interesting in the city. Some wished to get into a kindergarten with many children, and some with one child. The latter were the nervous young ladies who could not tolerate children's noise.

One doll was silent and did not say anything.

"Well, you, Gerda, where do you intend to direct your steps?" dolls asked from all sides.

"I would go back to my former doll Mama, back from where Knecht Ruprecht brought me to let me grow new hair. I have such a longing for small Annemie and vice versa. I was her youngest, and we were dear to each other," whispered the doll intimately.

"But if Knecht Ruprecht takes you someplace else?" said the proud doll in the pink silk dress.

"Then I will certainly die longing for Annemie," the doll sighed frightened.

The angel outside on the carriage seat had heard the voices of the dolls clearly. The loving words of the last doll warmed her heart despite the fierce winter cold.

"We will certainly ensure that Knecht Ruprecht brings you right back to your little Mama Annemie, you brave doll child," said one.

Knecht Ruprecht stopped, drew his large binoculars out of his coat and peered through them.

"My word, we must hurry, in all the nurseries a company sits at the windows and looks out for me. Heavens, it's fifteen minutes to Christmas. Forward!"

Once more the cloud-sled roared through the snow country.

Yes, in all nurseries, small noses pressed expectantly against the windowpanes.

Only Doctor Braun's Nesthäkchen had no time for gawking. The doll mother herself had her hands full to prepare the presents for her children. They were now all shut out of the nursery. With Hanne, outside on the window cupboard they crouched. Kurt and Lolo breathed peepholes in the icy floral pattern of the window glass, Irenchen and Mariannchen exchanged views about what had happened to sister Gerda, and small Babychen wondered excitedly whether she would get short dresses for Christmas.

Inside the nursery her mother, with hot cheeks, bustled back and forth. In the middle of the white table Annemie set the cute dolls' Christmas tree. On it she hung colorful sugar cookies. Fräulein had already fixed white wax candles that emitted magnificent Christmas light on the green branches. Annemie brought six dishes from her kitchen, and laid on them tiny doll doilies. The good Hanne had baked pastry, at Nesthäkchen's request. Her children would see small slices of gingerbread, a spice cookie, a piece of marzipan and colorful bowls.

Around the table Annemarie placed the plates, one, two, three, four, five, six. Yes, for whom should be the sixth? Outside at the kitchen window, five doll children waited for their gifts.

With special attention, Nesthäkchen placed on the sixth plate a marzipan pretzel, which she stroked maternally.

"So, my Gerdachen, this is for you, you shall not go empty-handed if you come back to me. I've asked every evening that dear God sends you to me. And Fräulein says Christmas returns all the dolls to their mommies who have been good to them. I was not bad to you, was I, my Gerdachen? I have even cut off my braids for you!" The girl ran her hand across her short haired curly blond head.

Annemie hurried to her cupboard and rummaged dearest things that she had made in kindergarten for her dolls. Oh, how diligent Nesthäkchen had been.

There was a tasteful carpet for the dollhouse, braided with colored ribbons, for Irenchen. Mariannchen got a small pearl bag for her handkerchief. Kurt received a silver paper slipper, just one, because he lost the second one. For Lolo the doll mother had strung a blue pearl necklace and another for Baby of red coral. In Gerda's place Annemarie put a necklace of gold beads and a silver bracelet.

The doll settings were complete, but youngest was not yet finished with her gifts. She had worked her industrious fingers for all.

On the nursery table, presents arrived for the big people. The red and gold striped bookmark would go to Grandma, and the blue silver checkered one next to it was for Aunt Albertina, because she should not be forgotten on Christmas Eve. For Mommy, Nesthäkchen had braided a cute basket and for Fräulein a napkin ring. Father got a calendar in leather that Annemie had framed with red silk. Brother Hans got an ink wiper with black silk, so that no one saw the blobs. Even for Klaus his good sister had worked, though he always annoyed her. She had made a magnificent back strap of colored wool and hollowed cork with Aunt Martha. Even Hanne and Frida, who were always so nice to the kids, were not allowed to go away empty-handed. They got cardboard pictures for their room, Frida the fidget from the Struwwelpeter, and Hanne the Soupy Kaspar, because Kaspar was as perfectly round as she herself. Annemie's last gift was a necklace made of colored beads, which would go to Puck.

Now the cabinet was empty, and that was good. It was high time. Outside the house, on the snowy front yard, Knecht Ruprecht's carriage had halted. Bustling, the angels unloaded all sorts of gifts and carried them into the house. An angel sat enthroned on the box, muffler over her nose. The coachman impatiently smacked his silver whip. Wow, weren't they finished yet? They had to get going!

"Did you leave me the doll for Annemarie, you angelic brat?" muttered Knecht Ruprecht, as the porter returned puffing and panting.

"We'll have to bring her the doll first, because the doll had such a longing for her little mamma," said the angel zealously.

Bells ringing, Knecht Ruprecht's sled whizzed off.

Ting-a-ling, the bell rang at the doctor's door that had been closed all day. Hans, Klaus and Nesthäkchen jumped into the Christmas room.

The Christmas tree flared, flashed and glittered with many, many lights. Annemie was so dazzled and dazed that she could initially distinguish nothing at all.

Klaus, who had recently begun piano lessons, sat down at the piano and Hans picked up the violin. The two boys, as a Christmas surprise, played "Silent night, holy night." Annemie sang along brightly.

Suddenly she stopped.

From the branches of the Christmas tree waved a doll's arm, over which peered a roguish face.

"Gerda, my sweet Gerdachen." In the middle of the carol, Annemarie's exclamation resounded joyfully, and no one could stop her.

The doll mother pressed her absent child to her heart and covered her joyful face with hot kisses during the Christmas song, which ended without Annemie.

"Are you back, my darling? Where were you stuck so long? Have you not worried about your mother?" whispered Nesthäkchen.

Doll Gerda made a mysterious face. Where had she been so long, eh? She told her mom during the evening in a dream.

"Silent Night" had died away, and Fräulein pushed Annemie to recite her poem, which she had learned in kindergarten, for her parents.

But Nesthäkchen had forgotten her Christmas poem. Gerda was back. She knew nothing else.

"Well, Lotte, you like your child now?" asked Mommy. "You have seen that your child has grown pigtails on her head?" Mom smiled at the soulful reunion of the two.

No, Annemie had not noticed. Correct! Gerda was no longer bald. Two handsome blond braids hung at her back, replacements for the ones her mama had truncated. So the sacrifice had not been in vain! And she wore a new dress of pink batik with a green sports jacket and cap. "Oh, Granny certainly knit that for me." Filled with impetuous gratitude, Annemie and Gerda hung on Grandma's neck, almost sending the old lady flying into the air!

"I have something Knecht Ruprecht has given you, darling," Grandma said when she had recovered her breath, and pointed to Nesthäkchen's gift table. There he was, the Lord Lieutenant, a large doll. He wore a fine uniform, and he presented his rifle at attention before Annemie.

"Oh, fine! Knecht Ruprecht thought that I am a boy, because I have no more braids," shouted the girl, the Lord lieutenant on her left arm, Gerda on her right. Annemie gave the soldier a tender kiss.

"Well, you're half a boy too, Lotte," teased father.

Annemie found time to admire her gifts and to thank her parents from the heart. Although no small clinic or small department store was there, she could be pleased with the beautiful gifts. Even new short dresses for Babychen that Fräulein had tailored.

But the best was and remained Gerda and the Lord Lieutenant.

"He shall defend my dolls when Klaus makes war against them," Annemie said eagerly.

Doll Gerda nodded pleased. She had a knight who would protect her against her enemy Klaus, moreover, one with a gun. Admittedly, Hanne got into a dispute with her cavalier, because he wanted to go out next Sunday with the pretty soldiers.

The good Hanne brought in a cute blue kitchen apron she made for Nesthäkchen, to go with the wooden clogs. Annemie said gratefully: "I lend you my lieutenant when you go out, Hanne. You have to be careful that you do not drop him, because you've broken so much crockery."

Aunt Albertina fetched from her capacious pearl bag a gift for Annemie. Slightly disappointed the girl looked it: a white ball of yarn with knitting needles.

"Are these perhaps for Grandma?" asked Nesthäkchen because Grandma was the only one who knit Annemie a stocking. No doubt, Aunt Albertina had made a mistake and given her grandma's gift. Auntie was so old.

But Aunt Albertina shook her head with its gray ringlets.

"No, my child, this is for you. A miracle ball it is. You'll have to learn to knit. If the yarn is knitted, as a reward something beautiful comes to light," said the aunt to her attentive niece.

"Oh, I will begin tomorrow. I'll knit a couple of nice stockings, aunt Albertina," promised Annemie.

"Just wait till you start school. You learn knitting, Annemiechen" said Fräulein.

"Nesthäkchen learns at grandma's, doesn't she, Luv?" said Grandma.

"I can learn in kindergarten. Aunt Martha has taught me to weave. Oh, my party!" Like a whirlwind Nesthäkchen was out the door.

She had forgotten about her own Christmas gifts for her children. The poor dolls were sitting in the dark kitchen, waiting for Knecht Ruprecht.

Fräulein lit the candles on the nursery Christmas tree, and the doll mother shouted so loudly that Irenchen fell on her back in shock. Then Nesthäkchen brought in all her children, and the adults came too.

It was a delight! Kurt threw his silver paper slipper into the air, and could not recover it; Irenchen admired her carpet so excitedly that she got blood red cheeks. Mariannchen tore her long-glued-shut eyes open, because she wanted to see what Annemie had brought her. Babychen tried the new coral necklace, and Gerda clung gratefully to her hardworking mother. Lolo looked enviously at Gerda, because she got a gold chain. Lolo came too close to the Christmas tree and scorched her black curly head.

Now the adults had their turn. Everyone admired Nesthäkchen's diligence, most of all Grandma; that's what grandmothers always do.

Puck and Klaus had confused their gifts. Klaus tied the pearl necklace around his left arm, because he wanted to look vaccinated like Hans, and Puck happily crunched Annemie's beautifully crafted horse leash.

Nesthäkchen remembered her Christmas poem. She recited it in a loud clear voice and got a kiss from Father. From Mom and Grandma she got two kisses.

The Christmas lights were low, they got smaller and smaller, and Nesthäkchen's eyes became small and smaller. Fräulein brought the tired child to bed. But before that, there was one surprise left. The good Fräulein had created from a basket a lovely crib for Gerda.

Today Annemie did not separate from her child. Gerda walked into bed with her and told her little Mama about her dream of Knecht Ruprecht's beautiful doll country where she had been so long.

The lieutenant stood all night on guard.

Chapter 19.
The new school satchel

The dear sun had melted the snow. The stone fountain cherub in the yard had trampled out his white snowy fur that he wore in winter. He stood as a naked boy. From the earth the first green blades of grass peeped out. Soon Annemie could play in the park again.

But she liked it well at home. Upstairs new tenants had moved in. Annemie could see into the nursery, which housed three cute children with dolls and hobby horses. The biggest girl was Annemie's age.

The girls nodded, of course, and often showed each other their dolls at the window. But they had never spoken to each other, although Nesthäkchen asked Mommy whether they could visit. Mom wanted none of it, because she did not know the parents of the girl.

"Finish up with Fräulein, Lotte, I want to take you with me," Mom said one day.

"Don't I go today to Aunt Martha's kindergarten?" asked Annemie surprised.

"No, Lotte, today we have something much more important." Mommy made a mysterious face.

"Oh, please, please, beloved, only mom, tell me what it is," tormented the curious girl.

But Mom just smiled and gave away nothing, although Nesthäkchen bombarded her on the way with questions.

They walked in the park a short distance, then on a long road, and now they were standing in front of a tall red building with a high wall.

"Here's the prison?" Nesthäkchen grabbed anxiously for mum's hand and tried to hold on to it.

"No, it's not quite so bad," laughed Mutti. "That's your new school. I want to take you to report to the Director, Lotte."

Distrustfully Nesthäkchen gazed for the first time at the school. It was recess. In the broad yard many girls of assorted sizes wandered around, merrily chattering and laughing, eating their breakfast bread. The petites had teamed up to form a circle and played "cat and mouse."

The uneasy feeling that stalked small Annemarie at the sight of the high wall disappeared. Oh, how nice it was here, almost as beautiful as Aunt Martha's kindergarten.

"I want to play!" Nesthäkchen released mom's hand and ran toward the circle of children.

But Mommy caught the runaway.

"Later, when you're a real schoolgirl, you must play, now we have to meet the Director. Do not be shy, Lotte, and give your best answer when he asks you a question."

"I will not be so stupid and shy," said the daughter eagerly.

The director was a friendly gentleman with a gray-black beard. He resembled father and liked Annemie immediately. He kindly said, "So this is the new pupil. What's your name, my child?"

"Annemie," answered Nesthäkchen loudly and made him her finest curtsey, "but if I'm good, I'm Lotte."

"Hmm, for us, Annemarie is sufficient," the Headmaster smiled. "And what is the surname?" He turned to Mother.

"Annemarie Braun," the latter replied.

"Date of birth?"

Before Mom could answer Nesthäkchen proclaimed beaming, "April 9th is my birthday. I wish to get from my grandma a school satchel and a shaving kit for my Lord Lieutenant, because Klaus has painted a beard on him, and in the afternoon there is chocolate with whipped cream!"

"That's beautiful," the nice director laughed properly. Then he listed the year of birth, the status of the father and the apartment.

Meanwhile Annemie had whispered something pleadingly to Mom, but she shook her head defensively.

"Would you like anything else, my child?" asked the Headmaster.

Nesthäkchen flapped her blue eyes innocently at him.

"I want so terribly to sign up my Gerda for school; she has two long braids and a school skirt."

"Well, your sister is probably too young to go to school; she must be as big as you are." The Headmaster patted her cheek kindly.

"But Gerda is not my sister," Annemie laughed aloud, despite Mommy's attempts to silence the blabbermouth.

"Gerda's my most recent, my youngest, but she enrolled in kindergarten."

"For dolls we have no place. The class would get too crowded," the Headmaster said in a good mood. "Well, we'll see you on time, April 10th, at ten o'clock in the first grade. Work industriously. Adieu, madame, adieu, my child."

Annemie curtsied, and then they were standing outside in the long corridor with many doors.

"You were not well-behaved," Mom began when they were back on the street, dissatisfied. "How could you be so cocky!"

"But the Lord Director kept asking." Nesthäkchen twisted her whiny mouth. "And if he does not want my Gerda, then I don't go at all in the ol' school! Without Gerda it's no fun for me! "

"School is not for fun, Lotte. You'll study diligently. You won't remain a pint-sized silly," Mom said earnestly.

April 9th came. On Nesthäkchen's birthday table were seven candles. In the middle a light of life flared, next to the new brown satchel from Grandma. Annemie was pleased about school. Ah, the pretty reader with pictures, the fine pen case which closed so humorously. And a pen box was there, just like the one Klaus had. A small black cat was an ink wiper, plus a pen and a long red pencil. Annemie did not rest until the new green plaid school dress could be fitted. It was tied to the black school skirt which was much finer than Gerda's. The leather breakfast box, or as Klaus called it, the "feed drum," was hung nearby; and last, strapped shut, the new schoolbag. So now the little schoolgirl was finished.

First she went to father's office, which was fortunately devoid of patients.

"Father, I am now a real schoolgirl," and the schoolgirl was sitting with her satchel on father's knee.

"Oh, I can not let you ride on my shoulders. I am sorry, a schoolgirl is too big," Father said with a smile.

The birthday girl looked thoughtful.

"Oh, you know what, Daddy, today you can give me a ride. I'm a real schoolgirl tomorrow." Annemie, who liked riding on father's shoulders, was happy to find a way to have another gallop.

A few seconds later you could see something strange. Doctor Braun jumped, trotted and cantered through the entire apartment. A schoolgirl rode on his shoulders with her satchel strapped on and exulted: "Gee" "Hott" and "brrr".

"So, that was my last performance." Father was breathing heavily and allowed the small rider to descend. "Starting today we're done with horseback riding!"

"But my Gerda can still ride you. She has not been accepted at school," the girl said.

Father promised.

"Mommy, who's going to sweep away the crumbs from the coffee table and scatter them for the birds on the flower board? Every day I have to go to school." said Annemie, proudly marching with her satchel up and down.

"Yes, it will be a problem, my Lotte." Mommy pulled Annemie's blond head toward her closely, so Nesthäkchen should not see how hard it was for Mom to give her child to the school.

Nesthäkchen raced into the kitchen.

"Frida, Hanne, have you seen my new satchel"?

"Wow!" said Hanne and forgot in sheer admiration to shut her mouth again. "I must bake pretzels for your birthday cake today, bigger than usual, right, Annemiechen?"

"Yes, schoolgirls are doubly hungry," the girl agreed seriously.

"But Annemie, you can not go to school yet," teased Frida, "who helps me in the morning to clean up? The carpet machine does not run without you."

"I need you to haul," interrupted Hanne, "if you do not come with me, to who should the merchant give the candy?"

Most affected was Annemie. Yes, really, she could not go to school, she had too much to do at home, school was not necessary.

When she entered her nursery, her dolls all sat with posies in their hands. Fräulein had arranged for them to congratulate their mom and show Nesthäkchen how indispensable she was. What should become of her children when she went to school?

"It's a pity about the beautiful new satchel," she said after careful consideration, "but I can not do a favor for the Lord Director and go to school tomorrow. Mom, Hanne and Frida need me, and my dear children would be left alone. Puck and you, Fräulein, you guys do not know what you shall do without me."

"Well, for your children I might worry, Annemie. I have to do the same thing," laughed Fräulein. "And Mom, Hanne and Frida have to see that they cope without you. Everyone must go to school and learn something, otherwise she remains stupid and everybody laughs at her."

Nesthäkchen did not want to be a laughing stock.

"It does not help my Gerdachen, but I have to go to school tomorrow," she sighed, taking her favorite on her arm.

With undisguised admiration Doll Gerda looked at the new school binder. The other dolls were amazed at their Mama, the schoolgirl.

"What are you going to do without me, Gerdachen?" whispered Annemie in the doll's ear.

Gerda made a sad face.

"You could perhaps go with Hanne and take my candy from the merchant," mused youngest.

Doll Gerda's face brightened.

"You can go alone to Aunt Martha in kindergarten. She was always nice to you. I promise to visit often." The girl kept on thinking.

Her eyes fell on the Lord Lieutenant with the handsome mustache who looked earnestly at both.

"Wait, I've got it, you are marrying the Lord Lieutenant. We'll have a wedding, Gerda. Your groom is waiting. You'll have a husband and will be no longer alone, if I have to go to school!" cried Nesthäkchen suddenly delighted.

Gerda laughed. A more beautiful man she could not desire. The lieutenant shone more briskly than usual because Gerda was a lovable doll girl.

Irenchen looked enviously at the two; she would have liked the pretty lieutenant for a husband.

"Yes, Irenchen, you shall have a wedding because you're my oldest," said the doll mother, who noticed Irenchen's lachrymose expression. "I don't have a lieutenant for you anymore, just my Kurt, but then you've got a husband, at least, even if his legs are kaput."

Irenchen nodded comforted, because she saw that Mariannchen was jealous of her Kurt. But for Mariannchen Nesthäkchen did not have another husband. Puck maybe, but Mariannchen would not have him because he was such a rowdy fellow and always snapped. He would certainly continue snapping and biting his wife.

In the afternoon, when the birthday chocolate was drunk with whipped cream, Nesthäkchen celebrated in her nursery a dolls' wedding.

The two brides were given white dresses, Gerda the pink sash, and Irenchen the blue dress sash. As a train Annemie stuck a handkerchief in the dress, because a bride must have a train. From Mother, Nesthäkchen had begged an old, white veil which was faithfully divided between Gerda and Irenchen as bridal veils. Frida had braided her two wreaths. There was no myrtle; she had substituted green parsley, but it looked just as good. The Lord Lieutenant and Kurt wore parsley bouquets in their buttonholes. Although Kurt appeared torn up for a groom, Annemie made him an impeccable helmet from newsprint because the lieutenant wore a soldier's cap.

The bride's carriage drove up, the white doll carriage. Annemie had harnessed Klaus' rocking horse to it. Solemnly they went to the church. On the front seat the was the Lieutenant with his Gerda, in the back seat was the second pair of newlyweds, Irenchen and Kurt. The latter looked sad. It was hard to abandon his carefree life and become a husband.

Mariannchen and Lolo contributed their trains to the brides, and Baby strewed flowers. Nesthäkchen administered the vows.

"Would ye marry, all four?" she asked the newlyweds.

And since none of them said "No," she continued: "The rings" and pulled out curtain rings as wedding rings for their hands. The marriage was solemnized.

Now for the wedding banquet: The bride mother set the table herself with her most elegant doll service. All dolls invited to the wedding took their places, and could taste the leftover whipped cream.

Kurt, the wild groom, jumped with his severed leg into the whipped cream. Irenchen, now his wife, dried him carefully with her handkerchief train.

Annemie brought drinking water to toast the health of the newlyweds, and all clinked coffee cups, as no glasses were available.

Klaus dragged in his barrel organ and started playing it. Everyone began to dance.

Each groom hopped around with his bride, and Annemie danced with Puck.

The wedding was over. The seven-year-old Nesthäkchen, tired from the beautiful day, went to bed.

"Tomorrow I'll be in school," she thought, "Oh, how glad I am that I have fed my children so well!" Nesthäkchen fell asleep.

But in her dream Annemarie could hear quite clearly how the barrel organ started to blare by itself. Oops, what was that?

The lieutenant put his hand to his cap and saluted his wife Gerda. They both hopped off together at a gallop.

Kurt made before Irenchen a bow and began to turn with her. He danced the tango despite his severed legs. The other dolls awakened and joined in the wedding dance. Mariannchen and black Lolo, even Baby, all skipped through the nursery.

Nesthäkchen's new satchel was ready for tomorrow. The satchel had made such a serious face throughout the day, and now was infected by the general mirth.

The satchel jumped off the table, in the midst of the dancing dolls. Clearly the girl saw the satchel in her dream. The satchel began to spin, she danced, and finally she hopped highest of all. The pen case jumped back and forth, and the pen sleeve danced with the black ink wiper.

The whole rollicking company cavorted in the moonlight, while Annemie slumbered on her first day of school.

*

Yes, she is still asleep, our youngest, and when she wakes up, she no longer has much time for her dolls. She's become a schoolgirl. But of that I'll tell you in the next volume.

Made in the USA
San Bernardino, CA
16 March 2019